BURNING SAINTS

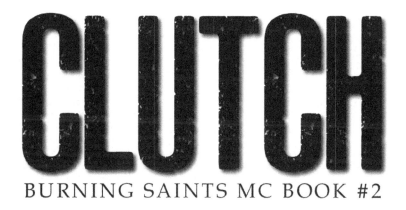

CLUTCH

BURNING SAINTS MC BOOK #2

JACK DAVENPORT

Clutch is a work of fiction. Names, characters, places, and incidents are the products of the author's imagination and are used fictitiously. Any resemblance to actual events, locales, or persons, living or dead, is entirely coincidental.

Cover Art
Jack Davenport

TRIXIE
PUBLISHING

ISBN-13: 9798614747466

Printed in the USA
All Rights Reserved

Oh, good gravy, this book is good. And I'm not just saying that because he does other amazing things with his fingers!
~ Piper Davenport, Contemporary Romance Author

Talk about getting my motor running!!!! (Get your mind out of the gutter. I was referring to all of the drama, suspense, budding romance, forbidden love.) Jack Davenport maybe a recent addition to the world of publishing but he has done an amazing job of entertaining, story telling, and creating fantastic characters. I can't wait to see what the future holds.
~ Trudy D.

For Deputy Aiello
Thanks for always having my back!

ONE

BURNING SAINTS

Clutch

MY PLAN WAS total dog shit, and Minus would never go for it, but at least I had something to bring to the meeting. Mr. President had made it clear during our last conversation that showing up empty handed wasn't an option. Jase 'Minus' Vincent was the newly minted president of the Burning Saints Motorcycle Club, and I was currently his Sergeant at Arms-length.

"You need another one of those, sweetie?" Sally Anne's smoky voice pulled me back from the haze I'd been lost in for God knows how long.

"I'm sorry, what?" I replied.

"Beer. Do you need another one?" she asked.

I needed another ten but knew "Good King Minus" would chew my ass if I showed up loaded. I downed the last swig from the bottle and pushed away my half-eaten burger and fries.

"No thanks, baby doll, I've gotta get to church," I replied, before grabbing my keys and putting my jacket on over my kutte.

"Okay, honey. Put this on the club's tab?" she asked, pointing to the wreckage on the table.

I smiled and nodded before heading for the door, happy to see it restored to its former glory, and in Sally Anne's sexy and capable hands.

Sally Anne's Place, our club's local watering hole, was once a respectable bar and grill, however, a while back, a rival club called Los Psychos took possession and turned it into a shitty pool hall called the Nine Ball. Los Psychos were a club of ex-cons who came up from Mexico and tried to make a name for themselves in the Pacific Northwest. They'd been gaining in numbers in Portland until their president, an asshole named Viper, made a series of miscalculated moves that left him, and his club's local presence, dead in a ditch courtesy of me and my crew. Any bastard Psychos who survived had been run out of town over six months ago.

The worst part of all of it was losing a brother in the process. In the end Grover chose to betray the Burning Saints, and Los Psychos killed him as soon as he was no longer of use to them. Still, Grover had run with my crew since we'd all been patched in together, and I missed him as much as I hated him for what he'd done.

I walked to my bike, Charlene, which was parked around back in a private lot reserved only for members of the Burning Saints, the only family I'd ever known; a family that had recently seen its fair share of drama.

I was promoted to Sergeant at Arms by the club's founder just before he dropped stone fuckin' dead. I don't mean to sound callous, because he was like a father to me, but my feelings about the man were currently a bit conflicted. Shortly before Cutter had been taken out by the big C, he'd named my best friend Minus as his successor. This was an unexpected move for several reasons, the least of which being Minus' banishment to Savannah, Georgia by Cutter himself. Minus was barely into his thirties and had nowhere near the experience level of some of the club's senior members. Shit, he wasn't even an officer before becoming president. Just a soldier who was banished to the wastelands. Now, I was supposed to kiss his ring. I didn't get it and I sure as shit didn't like it, and I wasn't the only one.

I kickstarted Charlene, and she came to life with a glorious roar. I headed north to the club's compound, which we called the Sanctuary. I'd hoped the ride would help to clear my head, but it was no use. I'd barely slept in weeks, was drinking too much, and was dreading going to church. I had a feeling that some of Minus' recent moves weren't going down well with some of the old school members, and that a few of them were ready to start pushing back.

Minus had always been my closest friend, but if the shit hit the fan, I wasn't sure if he'd have my back the way he used to back in the day. The Grover situation had me rattled.

I merged onto the freeway, signaled, and moved into the center lane after checking my blind spot. I got up to cruising speed and began thinking about my business proposal and how I was going to present it.

Holy fuck, business proposal. What the hell is going on here? Was I in a motorcycle club, or on Shark Tank? What the fuck came next? Selling Firefly lipstick on-line?

I'm not sure if, on his death bed, Cutter was trying to make good with Jesus or something, but in addition to the curious choice of naming Minus the new President, he'd also given him the task of turning the Burning Saints into a fully legitimate club that would no longer do illegal business of *any kind*. Minus was to take a gang of filthy one-percenters and turn them into a law-abiding, but still profitable, motorcycle club. To fuck things up even more, Cutter and Minus had hatched some hair-brained scheme that involved using Minus' girlfriend as some sort of public relations guru. The whole thing sounded like a fucking joke to me—like some sort of goddamn pyramid scheme—and I couldn't wait until Minus came to his senses and started running the club like Cutter used to. Or, at least, running it like an actual club. Minus was a smart motherfucker and I trusted him more than anyone, but I still felt uneasy as hell. I didn't know what he was thinking and he sure as shit wasn't sayin' much these days; at least not to me.

About half a mile from my freeway exit a dark brown Subaru wagon with a plastic kayak rack on top merged directly into my lane. It merged without any indication, causing me to swerve into the far-left lane, nearly losing control of my bike.

Motherfucker. As if I don't have enough to deal with today.

I steadied myself. "Hey, shithead! Open your fuckin' eyes!" I shouted and flipped him the bird, however, the clueless driver continued merging, still completely unaware of my presence, forcing me onto the shoulder. I revved my bike, but even Charlene's hellfire racket failed to get this checked-out dickwad to notice my presence. I stayed neck and neck with him, riding right alongside until I could see what had his attention; a cell phone in his lap. I was almost an organ donor because some hipster piece of shit needed to send a text to his fuckin' yoga instructor. Downward facing dipshit was about to find out that I was in no fucking mood for this shit.

I pulled in tight, right along his fuel-efficient turd wagon, and gave a swift kick to his side view mirror, which flew off and sputtered down the road behind him. He jerked the wheel and looked at me like he was gonna shit his pants.

"Ya see me now, fucker?" I yelled before delivering another kick, this time to the driver's side door. My blade-tipped boot cut through the door panel like butter. The driver sped up, signaled, and moved into the right lane.

"Oh, your blinkers *do* work, huh?" I yelled, grinning as I came in for another go at him. Then he made his final mistake. The little fucker turned his cell phone camera on me. I moved in, but he swerved violently into the right lane, narrowly missing another car. He then forced his way onto the far-right shoulder and slammed on the brakes. Maybe he thought if he stopped that I'd just keep on going but he was dead fucking wrong. I pulled over, set down my kickstand, grabbed a Mag-Light from one of my saddlebags, and walked quickly toward his car.

He kept his cell phone on me the entire time, shrieking like a little bitch, "I'm filming you! I'm filming *all* of this!" I could hear his pathetic wailing through the glass.

"Not for long, asshole," I said, and smashed his driver's side window with my flashlight, before reaching in and grabbing his phone from his hands.

"You can't do that!" he protested as I dropped it to the ground and gave it the heel of my boot, before kicking it into the flurry of traffic.

"That's a brand-new phone. You're gonna pay for that. And the damage you did to my car, you psycho," he wailed.

"I'm a psycho? Wrong pal. You're the fucking homicidal maniac driving a one and a half ton killing machine made of steel, plastic, and glass, without watching the goddamned road."

In perfect timing, a truck ran over the phone, instantly pulverizing what was left of it.

"I can't believe you did that—"

"You want me to pull you out of the car by your man bun and kick *your* dumb ass into oncoming traffic instead?"

"I'm gonna call the police," he continued to scream as cars zoomed by.

"Yeah? With what?" I grinned before reaching in and grabbing him by his jacket.

"Gimmie your fucking wallet," I demanded, and he did as he was told.

"Take...take my money. You...you can have ah...all of it," he stammered.

I let him go and pulled out only his driver's license, before tossing the wallet back at him. "I'm sick and tired of checked-out pieces of shit like you flying down the road without a fucking care in the world. I've visited too many hospital beds and gravesites because of you cell phone addicted, entitled mother fuckers."

The driver swallowed and looked down.

"Now I know who you are and where you live," I said, glancing down at his ID. "And if I or anyone from my club ever hears so much as a frog fart outta you, we're gonna come to your house, and make your face look worse than this car. Do you understand me?"

The petrified driver said nothing but nodded vigorously.

"Good. For now, I'm gonna let you off with a warning, Mister...Don Gaylor," I said, handing his license back. "But if I catch you texting and driving again..." I gave his front tire a kick with my weaponized footwear, puncturing it with a satisfying hiss. "Now, you have a nice fuckin' day, and be safe out there."

I strolled back to my bike, hopped on, and continued to church.

* * *

Gina

One more hour. One more hour. One more hour.

I repeated this mantra in my head until my breathing

and pulse returned to normal. I then stripped off my vomit-soaked jacket and tossed it into a large medical waste bag. No amount of dry cleaning in the world was going to return this unfortunate garment back to its former glory, and in all honesty, I probably should've retired it from my wardrobe years ago anyway. The projectile artist who had used it as his canvas was currently being attended to by my nurse, Maggie, so I had a few brief moments to clean myself up and get my head right before finishing his examination. My patient was a homeless man named Earl who came to my clinic at least twice a week.

Today, he'd gotten sick after eating seven fish sandwiches that he'd procured from a fast food restaurant's dumpster. This mixed with the half gallon of cheap red wine he drank, had caused a noxious eruption, the likes of which I'd never seen in my ten years of practicing medicine. I was quite sure I wouldn't be able to stomach even the thought of consuming seafood for at least a year.

I removed the only fresh set of clothes from my closet, a pair of jeans and one of David's old concert T-shirts, changed quickly, and reminded myself once more that in one hour I would be officially on vacation...and officially divorced. David and I had split up over a year ago, but today was the day the death of our marriage became official. Admittedly, as much as I still loved him as a friend, I felt a great sense of relief that I could officially move on from that painful chapter of my life. In celebration, I'd stocked up my Jeep with junk food, romance novels, gossip magazines, and a nice malbec, and was headed up to my father's old fishing cabin in Government Camp near Mt. Hood. It was the one place I could go to be completely alone, and God knows I needed to be by myself right now.

David Ellis was a good man, and a great cop, but he had been distant and emotionally unavailable as a husband. Not that I'd been much better as a wife. In all honesty, we had no business getting married in the first place, and likely had only done so because we were both naïve enough to believe that marrying your college sweetheart is simply what people were supposed to do. Perhaps *not* taking David's last name after we got married was a warning sign from my subconscious. Maybe more so was his complete lack of care when I gently broke the news that I wanted to stay with Gardner. Looking back, I think I wanted him to fight for me to take his name, but all he said was, "Suit yourself."

However, I *did* love him (at least I thought I did), but it was hard to tell at this point, as most memories of my marriage to him were tainted with disappointment and hurt feelings. To his credit, he tried to work on our relationship once I finally worked up the courage to tell him that I was unhappy, but all the couples counseling in the world wasn't going to change the fact that I didn't want kids, and he did. Nor would it change the fact that his job as a police officer was always going to come first. David had been painfully clear about this. He'd say things like "You want me to come home alive at the end of every shift, don't you?" To which I'd say, "Of course," so he'd retort, "Well then, I have to be a cop twenty-four-seven. That's the only way I can stay one step ahead of the bad guys and make sure I come home to you." Then he'd add, "And *someday*, to our family." This kind of talk would always lead to a huge fight, and eventually I wasn't sure I wanted him home at the end of his shift. It's not like I wanted him dead or anything, I just didn't want him home, or around me. Honestly, most of the time I didn't want *anyone* around me. I love my patients, my few close friends, and some of my family, but I rarely crave being around people. My mom used to call me shy, but that never sounded right to my ears even when I was little. I don't really like the word introvert either. It sounds so clinical and absolute. I just have a hard time being around people and sometimes wish I had more time to myself. This little getaway would be just what I needed to recharge my batteries, even if it was just a long weekend.

My office phone buzzed, and the voice of my nurse called out over the speaker. "Doctor Gardner, the patient in room four-oh-three is ready for you."

"Thank you, Maggie. I'll be right in," I replied.

One more hour. One more hour...

TWO

BURNING SAINTS

Clutch

"**Y**OU'RE LATE," MINUS growled as he stomped toward me.

"You set a new record. You didn't even let me finish parking before you started chewing my ass this time," I said, removing my helmet.

"I wouldn't have to chew your ass if you'd show up when you're supposed to."

"I hit a piece of trash on the freeway and had to pull over and deal with it," I replied, getting off my bike.

"I told you to be on fuckin' time, Nicky," Minus snapped.

"Nicky? Oh, a *formal* request; you must really need me. Well, excuse me your royal highness," I snapped.

"A *united front*, remember? That's what I said I needed today."

"Sorry I'm not meeting your expectations, bro."

"I fucking expect my Sergeant at Arms to be here." Minus sniffed me. "*Sober*, when I need him."

"*Your* Sergeant? Cutter made me Sergeant, not you," I blurted out, instantly regretting my words. Minus's face was a stone, but I knew him way too well to miss the hurt in his eyes.

"When's the last time you've been to the gym?" he asked.

"*What*?"

"The gym. When is the last time you sparred? I can always tell when you haven't trained in a while. You get all pissy if you've gone too long without hitting someone in the mouth."

"You volunteering, Mr. President?"

"Get the fuck inside and get your head on straight, *Clutch*," was all he said before turning and storming back inside.

The Chapel was the Sanctuary's main meeting hall, and where we held our all-club meetings and socials, like this weekend's all-club "picnic." Connected to the Chapel, was a smaller administrative room where we held "Church," our monthly board meetings. This was the time where only the club's officers, and sometimes other high-ranking Saints, would sit down to discuss the inner workings of club business. Until recently, that business largely involved collecting protection money, gambling debts, doing security for bad guys, shit like that. Our club was known as enforcers, leg breakers. The big scary dudes who could handle other big scary dudes. However, since Cutter announced his terminal cancer diagnosis and subsequent retirement, we were all living off a stipend, and were to "minimize illegal activity at all possible costs." Minus had assured us that more details would be coming our way at the next meeting.

"Thank Odin's dick, we can finally get started," Ropes, my oldest friend next to Minus, grunted as I entered the room. His brother, Sweet Pea, stayed silent and playfully flipped me the bird as I walked by. Every senior officer and captain was already there, and the mood in the room was far tenser than any meeting I'd ever attended. Not surprising given the circumstances.

"Now that our Sergeant at Arms is present, we can get started," Minus said as he stood at the head of the long boardroom style table that had been in this room for as long as the club had existed.

"I'm sure some of you have questions, and I appreciate you all giving me some time to sort all this shit out over the past months. I know everyone's business earnings have suffered, and that some of you have been taking shit from people on the street. Rest assured, I'm aware of your issues, and your problems will be dealt with accordingly," Minus said, addressing the room of stone faces.

"This club has never suffered like we did when we lost Cutter," he continued. "He was our founder, our leader, and like a father to many of us in this room. I'm grateful I got to spend his last few months here with him, and I'm honored that he's asked me to wear the President's patch. All I ask is that you give me some time to grow into it and trust me to guide this club into the direction that he and I worked to map out for us."

"Don't you mean you and your ol' lady?" Wolf, the club's Road Captain asked.

"Well, that didn't take fuckin' long did it?" Minus said smiling, slowly sliding his hands into his pockets. I knew from growing up with him that this was his move to keep his temper in check. Rather than make a fist, he'd put his hands in his pockets. Sometimes they'd stay there and sometimes they wouldn't, but he always tried the calm approach first.

"I'm glad you brought Cricket up, Wolf," Minus continued. "If you'll notice, she's not here, and that's the way it will stay. Despite what you may have heard, she's not co-captain of this club, nor is she an officer. She is, however, to be treated like any member of this club, and she is going to be working with us during this transitional phase. Cricket will continue to serve as a club advisor and community liaison—"

"*Lay on who?*" Wolf asked, to laughter around the room.

"She's our go-between with community leaders and shit," Warthog, the club's Chaplain said. "She's the one that's gonna make sure all of you assholes don't get locked up when the Sheriffs see you around town carrying TVs and microwaves."

"Why the fuck would we have all that shit?" Wolf asked.

"Because the Burning Saints now own a moving company, as well as several other legitimate businesses."

"So?" Wolf snapped.

"So, you and your crews are all expected to work at them," Minus said.

"The fuck we are," Wolf said rising to his feet.

"Sit down." Minus said, staring him down.

"Fuck this!" Wolf shouted. "I didn't join this club to lug sofas or work the counter at some fro-yo hut." Wolf seethed, not budging an inch. I stood up quickly, showing him that I had Minus' back. I may have been pissed at the guy, but he was my best friend.

"We gonna have an issue right here in the Sanctuary, Wolf?" I asked. His eyes darted to me, and he huffed before returning to his seat. I sat as well, happy that I didn't have to punch Wolf in the face. He could be a prick, but I liked the guy. He was loyal to the club and never personally gave me too much shit. He was old school, though, and I couldn't imagine him doing an honest day's work, no matter what Minus had planned.

"Let's get something clear right outta the gate," Minus said, his tone shifting. "The club's rules still apply. I'm the club's president and I will enforce them. If you wear a Burning Saints' patch, you are in this club for life." He looked around the room. "But, if you want out, feel free to leave right now," he said pointing at the door, before adding, "But you have to patch out."

"Look, Minus, I like you. You're a good kid, and for the record I voted against sending you off to Savannah, but you're not Cutter," Wolf said in a low tone, an angry scowl carved into his brow.

"No, Wolf, I'm not Cutter and I never will be, but make no mistake; I'm not a kid, I *am* this club's president," Minus said.

"We'll see," Wolf replied.

"You wanna patch out, Wolf?" Minus challenged. "Say the word and I'll have Warthog heat up the brand. Shit, you've been riding with the Saints for, what, eighteen years? I bet you've collected a lot of club ink over the years."

Wolf's jaw muscles tightened. Our club law states that any member who leaves the Burning Saints must have all club related tattoos blacked out via branding. All members have at least one club tat, and of course, most have several. Patching out has only happened twice in the club's history and I've only seen one. It was fucking brutal.

"You're playing a dangerous game, Minus," Wolf seethed.

"If you think this is a game to me, you don't know me at all," Minus said, approaching Wolf, who was still standing. When Minus reached him, he extended his hand. "Which is fair enough. I'm sorry, Wolf, let's start over."

The expression on Wolf's face was priceless. He looked like he was in shock, but he shook Minus's hand and quietly sat down.

"Good," Minus said with a smile and walked back to the head of the table. "You all know who I am, but it's probably fair to say most of you don't really know me. I've been gone for a long time, and a lot has changed in our world recently. I'm sure all of you are as confused as hell as to why Cutter chose me. Believe me when I tell you I was, too. I'd also like you all to know that I'm not confused now."

"Well, that makes one of you," Elwood, one of the club's oldest members said. "I'm still pretty fucking foggy on why we need to move away from enforcing and security, which are known money makers for us, and waste our time with moving companies and shit."

"Because, the times aren't changing anymore, they've already changed," Minus said. "We can't do the things we used to do and expect the same results. The Saints don't have the juice with the local PD that we used to. We simply can't pay off this new breed of cops as easily. There are too many security measures and pressure from top brass. Most of the money that used to be on the streets is now on the dark web, and gambling's now as close as the nearest Indian casino. Let's be real here. The club's income is one-third of what it was fifteen years ago. Club members are harassed by Portland's finest more than ever. There's a camera on every street corner and on every nosy citizen's cell phone. The streets are simply dead fishing grounds for us and most of our kind."

"So, you expect us all to go straight just because the streets have tightened up? Or because it's a big scary world out there where we might get hurt or arrested?" Elwood challenged. "I think we're all well fuckin' aware of the risks of being in an MC by now."

"And most of you have criminal records and have done time already," Minus said. "Is that how you want to spend the rest of your days Elwood? In a fuckin' cage? In case you haven't noticed, it's a "three strikes and your ass is gone" kind of world out there. These judges are handing out twenty-five years to guys just like you every day. Guys are doing serious time for low level shit, not to mention the kind of work we've been into. I'm gonna say it one more time. The old days are over. Clubs like the Dogs of Fire have figured out how to stay together as a pack and ride free without breaking the law. That's what Cutter wanted for his club and that's what I want for us as well."

"The Dogs ain't perfect," Wolf said.

"Nope, but they can help us, and we can help them, and with Cricket doing her PR magic in front of the City Council, Rotary Club, Portland PD, Fire, and whoever else she gets in her sights, the Burning Saints are going to become bigger and stronger than ever." Minus scanned the room, making eye contact with each member. "And we're gonna do it without spilling any more blood."

* * *

Gina

The moment I entered the first number of the code on the security pad to lock up the building, I heard the roar of motorcycles approaching the clinic.

No, no, no, shit, not now. I don't have time to pick buckshot out of a biker's hairy ass.

The Burning Saints were a local biker gang I had adopted, along with all the other neighborhood strays, while I was still an ER resident. As one would expect, these were big, scary dudes, but their president, Cutter was a teddy bear inside, and I was heartbroken about his recent passing. I always made sure my services and clinic were available to them, no questions asked. I'm not sure why, really, as they're all probably thugs, but I also saw a softer side to these men while they were in my care; well, some of them at least. I guess I just figured I'd rather patch them up, than have them bleed out from a knife wound. Besides, Cutter had always found a way to repay me for my services. I closed the cover on the keypad and walked to the glass front door just in time to see three of the Burning Saints park their bikes right out front. All I wanted to do was start my vacation, and my day had been filled with drama and vomit. Why not throw a pile of bikers on top?

"Hey there, Eldie, you still open for business?" Minus, the club's new handsome young president asked, smiling through the glass. If there had been any doubt in my mind that I was in fact the official physician of a biker gang, the reality that they'd given me a club name should have erased it. "Eldie," derived from L.D., which stands for Lady Doctor. This name was bestowed upon me by the departed Red Dog, one of the club's founding members and the very first Saint I'd removed a bullet from. Although, I was able to patch Red Dog up that night, I'm sad to say that road life caught up to him shortly after.

Standing with Minus were two other Saints, the aptly named Warthog, and Clutch, who scared me more than any of the Burning Saints. He never said much around me and always wore an intense scowl. He seemed like a man with a violent storm brewing inside of him, making me wonder just what kinds of things he was capable of.

Truth be told, my fear of Clutch came mostly from the fact I found him impossibly beautiful in every way. He was tall, with striking dark features, that tried, but failed, to hide an angelic face. To make matters worse, I saw him without a shirt on while the Saints were installing landscaping irrigation for the clinic last summer.

Clutch, and three other club members were working during an especially hot and humid day, and he'd stripped down to only his jeans and work boots. One sight of his muscular bare chest covered with his club tattoo gave me heart palpitations. I seriously thought I was going to pass out. I stored the image in my mind for future use.

"I'm actually trying to close up and get out of town for the weekend," I replied. "Is everyone okay? Is someone hurt?"

"No, we're okay, I just wanted to talk to you about setting up physicals for all the guys, and the clinic was on our way, so I thought I'd stop by," Minus said, still smiling.

I glanced at Clutch, whose eyes darted away the moment they'd made contact with mine.

"I can come back Monday," Minus said as he began to turn around.

"No, no, don't be silly. You're here now. Come in and let me turn my laptop on so we can get you on the schedule," I said as I unlocked the door.

"Eldie, I'll come back on Monday when you're back from your vacation," Minus said firmly but gently, putting a hand on Clutch and Warthog's shoulders. "My associates and I will leave you now with our apologies for delaying your travels."

Minus had a silver tongue and a slight southern drawl that was sexy as hell. I didn't find him quite as attractive as I did Clutch, but that's not to say he wasn't also gorgeous. It appeared for every Warthog of the club, the Saints also had a member who looked like they'd been chiseled out of a block of hotness. Perhaps I was just a little pent-up from the utter lack of actual sex in my life. I had packed both of my vibrators, and the latest book from Clay Morningwood, and was hoping to blow off some much-needed steam this weekend.

"Are you sure? I don't mind," I said, even though I really wanted to get out of there, but all three men were climbing onto their bikes.

Minus gave me a chin lift. "Goodbye, Eldie, have a great weekend."

I started to reply, but just then, Clutch did the unexpected...and smiled at me. The words coming out of my mouth stopped, and my expression must have made me look like a complete goober, because Clutch's smile dropped, and he quickly broke eye contact. Apparently, my game was so rusty I couldn't even properly return a biker's smile. This summed up my love life perfectly.

THREE

BURNING SAINTS

Clutch

ELDIE WAS MARRIED, so there was no way in hell I'd ever go after her, not that I had a chance anyway. Hell, I couldn't even smile at her without her face turning green at the sight of me. She was truly one of the hottest women I'd ever seen, and I swear she got better looking every time we crossed paths. When the club first met her, she was kind of scrawny, with big old nerdy glasses. Still cute as fuck, but not like now. Now she looked a lot healthier. All traces of the frazzled E.R. resident I'd first met had been replaced by a confident, fully-formed woman. She was also rocking a Roses for Anna T-shirt, these dirty librarian frames, and her hair was pulled back in a messy ponytail. I immediately thought of the fun the two of us could have with my hand firmly wrapped around it.

"She's too fine to be a doctor," I said to Minus as I got on my bike.

"She's off-limits Clutch," he replied sternly.

"I know, Minus. She's married. I don't fuck around with people's families. You know that," I said.

"It's not just that. She's our doctor, and I can trust her not to go to the cops or rat us out if she sees or hears something while treating one of us. I don't want you and your dick messing that up. She's too important to the club."

"I already said I'm not making a move," I snapped.

"Yeah, but you've also commented on how fine she is, and don't think I didn't catch you grinning at her," Minus said.

"Fuck you. I can't smile at someone now?"

"You can, but your smiles always come with strings attached," Minus said, starting his bike before I could respond.

As we rode on, and the sky began to darken, I replayed the day's events in my mind. After the heated discussion about the direction of the club, this weekend's club picnic should prove interesting, to say the least. Hell, with Wolf flexing and Elwood basically calling Minus a chicken, I was morbidly curious to see how the next forty-eight hours would play out.

Warthog and I still had a few stops to make in preparation for the weekend's festivities, including stopping at Charlie's Market to pick up a large booze order. Ropes and Sweet Pea were supposed to meet us there with a truck. Minus split off and headed back to the Sanctuary, and his absence caused me to breathe easier, which seemed fucked up to me.

We rode down Burnside toward Charlie's, with Warthog leading the way. About a mile down the road, I caught sight of a powder blue Jeep in my mirror that I immediately recognized from Eldie's parking lot. It was closing in on me fast and changed lanes at the very last moment in order to pass me on the right. I looked over to see Eldie behind the wheel, arms flailing, singing at the top of her lungs, completely unaware that I was next to her. I sped up to stay beside her and could then hear "In the Air Tonight" by Phil Collins blasting from the Jeep. Eldie was spastically thrashing her arms about with every epic drum fill while simultaneously attempting to belt out the lyrics. I suddenly saw her stop, only to open a bag and retrieve a chocolate frosted treat which was promptly stuffed into her mouth.

However, before she could finish chewing, she glanced over to find me gawking at her from my bike. A look of horror crossed her face and she released a muffled scream before yanking the wheel hard right and gunning the Jeep into the far-right lane. She blew right through the lane, hit the curb, and a no parking sign with enough force to pop one of the Jeep's front tires and deploy the airbag.

"Holy shit! Eldie!" I pulled over, jumped off my bike and ran to the Jeep, Warthog behind me moments later. I opened the driver-side door to find a stunned Eldie, her face partially covered in white powder from the deployed airbag. Her glasses were crooked and broken, the chocolate treat still in her mouth.

"Jesus, Eldie, you okay?" I asked, checking her over.

She tried to speak before chunks of slobber and half chewed donut came pouring out of her mouth, running down the front of her shirt.

She gasped as she clumsily wiped her mouth with her bare arm. "Oh my god!"

"Is anything broken? Are you okay, Doc? Are you paralyzed? Can you wiggle your toes, do you smell burning toast?"

"That's a stroke symptom," Eldie said, through chocolate brown teeth.

"Here, sweetie, let's get you outta there and cleaned up. I'll get a brother to come and tow your car, and we'll get this damage taken care of, and get your Jeep back on the road," I said.

"What? No, you don't need to do that. This was all my fault," she said, still a bit dazed.

"No shit this was all your fault," I said with a laugh. "But I'm gonna take care of you until your ol' man can come get you. Come on, let me help you out of there. Careful, I've got you."

I helped her to a nearby bus stop bench and sat her down. Warthog laid out road flares and directed traffic while I called for an ambulance.

"No, don't do that, I'm fine, really," Eldie protested.

"Tell you what. Since I'm not a doctor, and the only doctor I know just got hit in the face pretty good, how 'bout we let the EMTs decide if you're okay," I said, handing her a clean bandana from my pocket. "Here, you've got some chocolate on your chin."

"Oh God, I must look like a maniac. I honestly don't know why I did that. You just…scared me…I guess," she said sheepishly.

"Scared you?"

"I don't know," she said, to the sounds of approaching sirens. "What am I gonna tell the police? They're gonna take me to jail and lock me up for driving like an idiot."

"Don't worry, Doc, I've got you. I'll take care of everything. Just stay right here and let me do the talking."

* * *

Gina

I was in shock, and not just because of the airbag to the face.

What the actual fuck was wrong with me? Why did I freak out like that?

I was absolutely mortified. I seriously contemplated

getting up and throwing myself into oncoming traffic out of sheer embarrassment. One moment I was zipping down holiday road, me and Phil were singing, a bag of Mr. Winston's chocolate Yum Yums to keep me company all the way to the cabin, then next thing I knew, hottie biker boy is staring at me, and I'm up close and personal with city property.

I can't believe he was watching me doing my best/worst carpool karaoke. I can't believe he saw me stuffing my face with chocolate Yum Yums.

A large delivery truck approached.

I mean, seriously, the pain of hurling myself in front of that thing couldn't be worse than what I'm feeling right now.

I didn't know why I was so mortified that Clutch had seen me being goofy. If it had been some random stranger who'd busted me rocking out to a sold-out crowd at Dashboard Stadium, I would have been embarrassed, but I wouldn't have damn near driven off a cliff to break eye contact. This weekend was not going as planned. If there was even a weekend left to salvage. At this point, I should probably take this as a sign to stay home, but that was the very last place in the world I wanted to be.

The ambulance arrived and the EMTs wheeled a gurney and back board to my bench.

"I'm fine, really," I said, starting to get up.

"Ma'am, please stay seated, you could have a spinal injury that you don't know about," one of the EMTs said.

"I'm a doctor. Really, I'm fine. Just some bruising to my face and ego," I said, trying to smile measuredly.

"Ma'am, please allow us to look you over and make sure you're okay, ma'am."

"Okay, fine just enough with the ma'am," I snapped.

"Sorry, Doctor," the EMT said sheepishly.

"No, that's not what I meant, never mind," I huffed in resignation and allowed the EMTs to poke and prod me until they were satisfied that I didn't need to go to the hospital. I eyeballed Clutch nervously as he spoke with the officer from the Sheriff's department who'd arrived. God knows what he was saying to him. As the EMTs packed up, the officer approached me, with Clutch directly behind him.

"Good evening, ma'am, I'm Deputy Aiello, sounds like you've had a bit of trouble tonight."

Great, time for more ma'aming.

"Yes, I guess so," I said, smiling nervously. Clutch was mouthing "don't worry" behind the cop's back.

"Did you get a good look at the driver of the other car?" he asked.

"The *other* car?" I stayed smiling.

"The one that ran you off the road. The brown Subaru. Mr. Christakos was able to give us an incredibly detailed description of the car but said he couldn't see the driver. Did you?"

"I'm sorry. I'm confused. Who's Mr. Christakos?" I asked.

"The gentleman on the motorcycle. He said he saw the whole thing, and that a brown Subaru wagon with a kayak rack on top ran you off the road and sped off. He said he knew you. That you were a doctor at a local clinic."

"Yes, yes that's right. I'm sorry, I'm just a little disoriented from everything," I said. Clutch was winking and giving me a private thumb's up while the cop scribbled notes in his logbook.

"So, did you?" The cop asked.

"Did I what?"

"Get a good look at the driver?" He looked at me blankly. "Are you okay ma'am? Do you need me to get the EMTs again?"

"No, I'm good, and its Doctor Gardner, Doctor Gina Gardner," I said.

"Speaking of identification, can I see your driver's license when you get a chance?"

"Oh, yes, of course. It's in my purse, which is in the car," I said, starting to stand.

"I'll get that for you!" Clutch said.

"Thank you, Mr. *Chriznowski*," I said, cringing on my own words. I could see Clutch look back at me, but without my glasses I couldn't make out his expression.

"Um, no, no I didn't see what he looked like." I said, returning my attention back to the Deputy.

"So, it was a man, then?"

I'm sure for Clutch, lying to the police was no big deal, but as someone who was until recently married to a cop, I was sweating bullets. I couldn't even remember the name Clutch had given the Deputy.

"No. I don't know. It could have been a woman. I didn't really see. It could have been a German Shepherd for all I know," I said, laughing nervously.

"Why would a dog be driving a Subaru?" he asked, flatly.

"Would that be odd? Do they usually drive Hondas?" I asked, then burst into hysterical belly laughs.

Pull it together Gina, this is not the time for one of your nervous giggle fits.

"Ma'am, have you been drinking tonight?" he asked, just as Clutch returned with my purse.

"No," I said, a little irritated by the question, but still fighting to hold back the laughter.

"I'm sure she's just shaken up from the whole thing officer," Clutch said, handing me my bag.

"Is there someone we can call to come get you? A family member or husband?" Deputy Aiello asked.

"Um, no. My…family is all out of town. I'm on my own tonight," I said, still getting used to how to announce my current status.

"Tell you what." Clutch said. "The EMTs gave the Doc here a clean bill of health, and we've got a tow truck on the way for her Jeep, so how 'bout once you're done collecting her information, I'll make sure she gets home nice and safe."

"Is that okay with you ma'am?" the Deputy asked me.

"Sure, that sounds good. Thank you, Mr. Chriz..."

"Christakos," he said smiling. Ohmigod his smile. When he smiled, every ounce of scariness melted away from him and my insides became gooey.

"I'm sorry, I guess I've only ever known you as Clutch," I said, apologetically.

I suppose, I'd always figured it best to ask the Burning Saints as few questions as possible.

"No need to apologize, *Gina*," he said with a wink.

Gulp.

I finished up perjuring myself with Deputy Aiello and, as promised, Mayday, the club's mechanic showed up to tow my Jeep off to their garage.

"You ready to hit the road?" Clutch asked.

"What? On *that?*" I asked pointing to his two-wheeled death trap.

"First of all, her name is Charlene and you'll hurt her feelings if you call her "that," and secondly, yes we'll need to ride Charlene to our next destination as my Bentley is currently in the shop next to your Jeep."

"You have a Bentley?" I asked.

Of course, he doesn't have a Bentley, it was a joke, you gullible goober.

Clutch smiled wider. "C'mon Doc, you'll be alright," he said, and extended his helmet out to me.

"I'm not sure about this," I said nervously approaching *Charlene*.

"It's okay, she don't bite...but I might."

I gave him a stern look, but the mere thought of him actually biting me anywhere made me shiver.

What in the name of Lisa Frank am I doing getting on a motorcycle with an actual biker? And why is the mere thought of Clutch biting me turning me into a cat in heat?

"C'mon, the others have a few stops to make, but you and I can head back to the Sanctuary," he said.

"The Sanctuary?"

"It's our clubhouse. It's also where some of the members live, and where the garage is located. You can sign the paperwork for your Jeep, and I'll make sure it's all taken care of, free of charge. Then I'll arrange a lift back home for you and your baggage."

"You don't have to do all that," I said.

"Sure, I do. After all, it was at least *partly* my fault you crashed," he said smiling. "If I hadn't interrupted your concert, you'd be wherever you were headed by now."

I felt my face get hot and knew I must be turning red.

"Hey, don't be embarrassed," he said lifting my chin. "You have some mad air drumming skills."

I smiled, blushing even more, and quickly turned my head away. "Okay, that's enough of that," I said sternly. "I appreciate the offer, but I think I'll just grab an Uber and meet you at your shop."

"C'mon Doc, don't be silly. Just hop on and we'll be there before you know it," he said sliding onto his motorcycle.

"I...ahhh..."

"Lemme guess," Clutch looked back at me smirking. "The good doctor has never been on a bike before."

"No, that's not true!" I squeaked defensively. "David and I rode Vespas in Italy on our honeymoon."

"You rode Vespas? Like, those little scooter things?" he asked flatly.

"Yes," I said, heat creeping up the back of my neck from embarrassment.

"Well then, I stand corrected. I didn't realize you ran with such a rough crowd, Eldie," he teased while I tried in vain to hide my smile. "Maybe you want to hop up front being as though you're such an experienced badass."

"Okay, so maybe I've never been on top of a real motorcycle before." I surrendered.

"On top of a motorcycle?" He burst out laughing and I was sure I must be beet red at this point. "First of all, baby, Charlene is a *bike*, and you ride *on* her."

"Don't call me that," I said.

"No, Charlene's the name of my bike, remember. I know your name is Gin—"

"Eldie is fine, that's not what I meant, and you know it. I meant don't call me baby."

"Sorry, Doc. I didn't mean anything by it. It's just kind of how I talk with the women who hang around our club. Sweetie, baby, sugar pie, they're terms of endearment to me, and to them."

"I'm not one of your hang-around girls, Clutch. I'm a doctor and a woman who expects to be treated with respect," I said sternly. Clutch's smile dropped completely, and traces of the man that scared me flashed across his deadly serious face. He got off his bike and stepped to me.

"Gina, I'm sorry if I offended you. I've always respected you and appreciated what you've done for our club. I know you don't really know me that well, or probably at all for that matter, but I guess I've just always considered you one of us. One of the Burning Saints that is."

The sincerity and softness in his voice did things to my mind, heart, and pussy all at once, and I needed that shit to stop right here and now.

"Please come with me. I promise I'll keep you out of harm's way, and that Charlene'll get us both home safely. You never know, you might end up liking the ride," he said softly.

Yeah, buddy that's the problem.

My under-stimulated loins were clearly going through some sort of mid-life, post-divorce crisis, and this scary bad boy was doing a number on me. But something inside of me also believed him entirely when he said everything would be alright, and before I knew it, my legs were straddled around Charlene, and my arms were wrapped tightly around Clutch as we sped into the night.

FOUR

BURNING SAINTS

Clutch

ELDIE CLUNG TO me around every curve, her glorious tits pressing against my back. There was no feeling in the whole world quite like it, and Eldie's body felt like it was custom made for riding with me. My cock was rock hard and felt like it was going to rip through my jeans. Having Charlene purring between my legs didn't help matters either. It was probably good that we reached the Sanctuary when we did, because thoughts of what I wanted to do with Eldie were about to distract me to the point of driving us both off the road. Eldie leapt off the bike and removed her helmet which had teased her chocolate brown hair into "fuck me" perfection.

"That was soooo much fun! Can we do it again later?"

she asked, clapping her hands rapidly.

"Yeah, sure, Doc," I said smiling. "We can go anytime you want."

"Is riding a...*bike* always that much fun?" she asked grinning.

"Look at you pickin' up the lingo, you're a real biker bitch now." I felt like an asshole the moment the words flew out of my stupid fucking mouth, and I quickly tried to take them back. "Eldie, I didn't mean—"

She was dead silent for several moments before bursting out laughing so hard I thought she was going to burst a blood vessel in her eye. She was in a full-on giggle fit for at least two minutes straight.

"I...can't...breathe...ohmigod," she said as she struggled for air. "If you only...knew how far from reality biker...bitch...is from the...real me."

"I don't know, Doc, you seemed to take to riding pretty quickly from where I was sitting."

"Thank you. I needed... a good laugh" Eldie said, using her t shirt to wipe the tears from her face, only then noticing the mudslide of chocolate and slobber that had stained the front of it.

"Oh gross! That's repulsive," she exclaimed.

"C'mon, let's get inside. We'll get you some water for your shirt, and maybe something a little stronger for you," I said, guiding her to the gravel path that lead to the Chapel building.

It was then that Eldie noticed the large group of Saints congregating.

"Are there always this many people here?" Eldie asked.

"Oh, shit. I almost forgot. This weekend is our annual club picnic," I said.

"Club picnic? As in there's a *bunch* of people here?" she asked as she ran back and checked herself in Charlene's mirror.

"You look great, Doc, don't worry about a thing," I said.

"I look like I just got back from an exorcism...," she leaned closer to the mirror, "...where I was the guest of honor."

"Wait a minute. I think I've got something you can change into," I said, remembering that I had several Burning Saints T-shirts in my saddle bag. Cricket had them made for us to give out to the locals on the streets. All a part of the horseshit campaign to soften our image. I handed Eldie a shirt, along with a bottled water.

"I figured you could use this to clean up."

She thanked me and looked at the tag on the back of the shirt.

"You don't happen to have one that's a size up from this, do you?" she asked, peering into the saddle bag which I quickly closed.

"Sorry, Doc, that's the largest size I have with me."

I stared right into her gorgeous brown eyes and lied. I had shirts one, two and three sizes larger in my bag, but I wanted to see Eldie wearing the size I'd selected for her. A size that I knew would hug every single one of her curves in just the right way. I knew I couldn't touch her, so I wanted to look as much as I possibly could.

"Can you, um...," Eldie said, motioning for me to turn around as she stepped over to a nearby tree.

"Of course," I said and did as I was asked.

I turned to face Charlene, my back now turned to Eldie and the lucky tree that kept her partially hidden. However, I could now see Eldie in plain sight through Charlene's side mirror as she peeled off her stained shirt. I knew the right thing to do was to look away, but when she unhooked her bra and let her tits free, my eyes stayed glued to that mirror. I'd honestly never seen a more beautiful pair of breasts in all my life. My raging hard-on came back with a burning vengeance, and the absolute torture of not being able to fuck her was starting to make me crazy. However, what she did next was simply next level in the cruelty department. She took her bottled water and slowly, carefully poured its contents down her chest, before gently rubbing herself down with the bandana I'd given her earlier. I stood transfixed, as she finished cleaning up before slipping the tight Burning Saints T-shirt over her large, bare tits.

"Okay, I'm all ready," she said after a few moments, and I turned around to face her, knowing full well if she'd looked down at my crotch, she'd see a bulge the size of an armadillo. The shirt did an even better job than I'd planned, not to mention the added bonus of her going braless. Eldie's hard nipples showed through the black cotton, and I could think of nothing more than having one between my teeth.

"You okay?" she asked. I assumed by her question that I was not hiding my expression well.

"Jesus, Doc. I was just kidding about the biker bitch thing. Maybe I do have more sizes, lemme just double check."

"No, I'm fine. Let's go. This is already the second time I've had to change my top today, and honestly the bra was still wet from the first time I had to wash it out in the sink. After the day I've had, it no longer matters. So, I'm gonna go to your little picnic with my puppies bouncing, and I don't give a shit," she said proudly.

"Do you wanna wear my kutte?" I asked,

"Yeah, that would be great," she said quickly.

"C'mon, Doc," I said, putting my kutte around her already shivering body. "We'll get you some proper clothes from one of the girls."

* * *

Gina

Walking back to Clutch, I bit the inside of my cheek to

keep from saying anything about his rather impressive erection. Good God, that thing could do some damage, and I kind of wanted to find out how much.

The little shit, trying to tell me he suddenly had more shirts. I knew he'd been lying the second he slammed the luggage thingy on his bike closed. One thing I knew about myself was I had a great rack and it wasn't lost on me that Clutch agreed.

So, now he was going to watch me in his tight T-shirt, sans bra, nipples hard enough to cut glass, and suffer.

I did appreciate him offering me his vest, though. Lordy, I was cold. I needed tequila, pronto…and food. In the warmth of a building.

Clutch led me inside and I couldn't help lagging behind. I was not a fan of people. I liked persons, but groups made me feel claustrophobic, and the large group of scary-looking bikers was suddenly making me nervous. Which I knew in my heart was stupid.

For the love of God, Gina. You've treated most of these guys for one stab wound or another, not to mention bullet holes, infected prison tats, and road rash.

"You okay?" Clutch asked, turning to face me.

"Yep," I said, with emphasis on the 'P.'

"Stick with me," he said.

"Your hand is like a vice grip," I pointed out. "I *am* stuck with you."

He grinned, loosening his hold. "Wine?"

"Tequila."

His eyebrows raised. "Yeah?"

"I'm a biker bitch remember?"

Clutch grinned. "Shots it is."

"And food."

"Burgers or dogs?"

"Both?"

He laughed. "C'mon. Let's get you fed."

I nodded and followed him into the fray.

Clutch led me to where Minus's girlfriend, Cricket, was chatting with a few of the club women in the kitchen.

"Gina?" she said, hugging me. "I almost didn't recognize you outside of your doctor's coat. You look adorable," she said.

I chuckled. "Thanks. It wasn't planned."

She smiled. "Heard you had a run-in with a pole."

"And a few chocolate Yum Yums, thus the shirt; courtesy of my new fashion coordinator." I motioned to Clutch.

"Ah." She frowned. "The shirt's kind of small. Do you want a bigger one?"

"Nope, this is good."

"Okey doke. You let me know if anything changes."

"I will."

Clutch returned with a plate full of food and I grabbed it from him, shoving the hot dog into my mouth. Clutch's eyes widened, and I decided to eat just a little slower, making his neck turn a very satisfying shade of pink as he watched my mouth slide over the dog before turning away and walking back toward the bar.

He grabbed a couple of glasses and a bottle of Patron and walked back to me with a look of smoldering hotness. Jebus, I wanted that face between my legs. I took a few deep breaths and refocused on my plate, which was now empty.

Of course, it was. One thing a lot of people didn't know about me, was that I could eat my weight in meat. So far, that ability hadn't caught up with me, but as I hurled towards forty, I anticipated that my weight would become a problem.

He raised the bottle of tequila and I nodded, so he set it on the kitchen island, pouring us each a glass.

Which we downed. "I love Patron."

He grinned. "Who doesn't?"

"Crazy people."

"Indeed," he said. "C'mon. I'll introduce you to a few of the guys you haven't met."

I took another shot, and then followed him into the great room.

I was introduced to guys with names like Ropes, Doozer...Ringo, I couldn't keep up. Through the haze of shots and new people, my short-term memory was getting spongy fast. Next to go would be my good judgement.

FIVE

BURNING SAINTS

Gina

I WAS TIPSY. Shit. Tipsy also meant I was horny. No, I should probably clarify. *Clutch* made me horny and the tipsiness lowered my inhibitions. God damn, I wanted to kiss every inch of his body.

He caught my eye and raised an eyebrow. I blushed and focused on the beer I was currently holding. Shit, when did I start drinking beer?

"You okay?" Cricket asked.

I glanced her way. "Hmm?"

"You're all flushed. Are you feeling okay?"

I forced a smile. "Oh, yes. Just warm from the alcohol, I think."

She frowned. "You might want to get some water."

"You know what? That's a great idea," I said. "I'll be back in a bit."

I set the beer on a table and headed into the building to get some water and perspective. I felt like my nerves were hovering at the edge of my skin and I needed to figure out how to ease the ache...or get the hell out of there. He was too close, too gorgeous, too... everything.

"Hey, Doc," Clutch said, his deep voice washing over me making my nether regions zing with need.

I squeezed my eyes shut briefly and turned to face him. "Hey, Clutch."

"You okay?"

"Yep. I was just grabbing some water."

"There's water outside."

"I know," I ground out.

"You need somethin' else?"

"Like what?"

He crowded me, and I stepped back...right into the kitchen island. "I don't know. Anything."

I licked my lips.

"Yeah, like that," he said, grinning as his beautiful face got closer.

"No, I'm good."

He leaned back slightly and raised an eyebrow. "I don't think that's entirely true, now is it?"

I studied him, the alcohol mixing with a sudden surge of adrenaline. "Anything, handsome?"

"Yeah, baby, anything."

I ran a finger down the corded muscle in his neck. "How do you feel about one-night stands?"

"I'm a fan."

"Yeah?"

He smiled, his eyes darkening with need. "Yeah."

"You got protection?"

"Do I look like this is my first rodeo?"

"Where's your room?" I asked.

"Wait." He stepped away. "You serious?"

I bit my lip. "Yes."

"I know you've had a few tonight, but aren't you forgetting about your husband?"

"Ex-husband," I corrected.

"What? As of when?" He asked.

"Today, as a legal matter of fact." I grinned.

"That's a big deal."

"Indeed." I ran my finger down his chest. "Some might even say it's a cause for a celebration…so?"

"Still can't do it, Eldie. Sorry, baby. I want to, but no."

Again, mortification hit me like a ton of bricks. "Oh, okay. No problem."

"Babe, don't do that. I'm not turning you down because I want to."

I chuckled, but I really wanted to cry. "Clutch. It's all good. Seriously. I'm a little tipsy, which makes me horny." I waved my hand dismissively. "Nothing a good vibrator can't take care of later."

Why the fuck did I just say that? He didn't need to know that. God! What the hell is wrong with me?

He looked a little surprised by my confession, so I smiled and patted his chest. "Close your mouth, big boy. You'll attract flies."

He gave me a crooked grin and crossed his arms. "We'll revisit this topic when we get to know each other better."

"Sure."

Clutch studied me a few seconds more, then headed toward the restroom.

I, on the other hand, grabbed my purse and called an Uber. Time to go home and hide in abject horrified embarrassment.

There was no way in hades I'd be able to face Clutch again, so, like the coward I was, I slid out the back. More of a slink, really, but cowardly, just the same. I waited until I was in the car before texting Minus to thank him for having me.

Letting myself into my condo, I belted out a frustrated groan and made my way to my bathroom. I needed a shower. Actually, I needed a shower and a vibrator. Not necessarily in that order.

I poured myself a glass of wine before I engaged in some much-needed relief, kicking my shoes into the corner of my bedroom. Feet finally free, I headed back the way I came and to my kitchen. I loved my home. It was probably bigger than I needed, with three bedrooms and three bathrooms, plus an office, but it was all me. I'd gutted the great room, which had a weird accordion partition between the kitchen and dated living room, opening the wall and installing a huge island to break up the space. Marble with distressed white cabinets had proven to be the perfect backdrop for my favorite color, red, accented throughout the space.

I had floor to ceiling windows that overlooked the Willamette River and a balcony big enough for a small grill, table, and two chairs. One day I planned to use that grill, but for now, it was there for show.

Sipping my wine, I stared out at the view for a few precious moments. I loved Portland. I loved the peace brought by the rain, and even though today was sunny, it wasn't hot.

I started toward my room again when the intercom buzzed, and I frowned. I wasn't expecting anyone, so I ignored it, but it sounded again, so I grabbed my phone and pulled up the camera.

Shit.

Clutch.

No.

Huh-uh.

Nope.

"Eldie, I know you're in there. Let me up," he said, his

face tipped to the camera.

Maybe if I stood perfectly still and remained quiet, he'd go away.

He smiled. Slowly. Lethally. "Gina, baby. Buzz me in."

I bit my lip. Hard. But it didn't stop the ache in my pussy at the sound of my name on his lips.

"I can wait here all night," he continued.

I tapped my phone to my forehead trying to think. What was he doing here? *Why* was he here? How the hell did he know where I lived?

These weren't the only questions that rattled through my head as I glanced back at my phone, but they were the most disturbing ones.

"I'm wait*ing*," he said in a sing-song voice.

I hit the green icon to buzz him in and walked back to my front door to wait for him to arrive. I didn't have time to check my appearance, but he wasn't going to be here for long, so it didn't really matter.

The knock came, and I pulled the door open, filling the space so he didn't feel welcome. "What do you need, Clutch?" I asked.

"Why'd you leave?"

"I was tired."

He frowned. "Are you feelin' the car crash?"

"No, I'm fine."

"Are you sure, Doc? Maybe you should ice or something."

Why was he being so sweet? I needed to shut this down, post haste. "Clutch. I'm good. How do you know where I live?"

"Don't think I should answer that."

"Probably not," I agreed. "Okay, I'm going to take a shower and then get an early night."

"You want some company?"

"No."

"You sure?"

I took a deep breath. Then another. "You said no earlier. Why the sudden need to stalk me and follow me home?"

"I said no, because we were at the club. Sacred land and all that. But I got to thinkin' about what you said, and then I couldn't think of anything else."

"Well, now that I've sobered up a bit, I've come to my senses."

"Drink more, then."

Goddammit, he was so fucking charming, I was back to wanting to kiss, and perhaps lick him all over.

"Yeah, that," he said. "I like that look. You gonna let me in?"

"I don't think—"

His mouth covered mine gently, and I dropped my phone as I grabbed his shoulders to stay upright. Holy shit! Of course, he could kiss.

I leaned back to create some distance. "If we do this. It's a one-time deal," I said. "No regrets, no emotions, and we never speak of it again."

"I'm good with that."

"I mean it, Clutch. No one can know about this."

He smiled, his hand sliding to cup my ass. "Lips are sealed, beautiful."

I nodded. "Okay."

He kicked the door shut, and then our mouths were on each other, frantic and passionate as he lifted me, so I could wrap my legs around his waist. "Bedroom?"

"End of the hall," I panted out, kissing him again as he carried me down the seemingly endless corridor.

Pushing open my bedroom door with his foot, he carried me over the threshold and set me on my feet. He removed his kutte, which I was still wearing, before tugging my T-shirt from my jeans and lifting it over my head. I grabbed for his jacket and pushed it off his shoulders, sliding my hands under his shirt and up his chest. "Off."

He grinned, reaching behind his neck and pulling it over his head. I nearly passed out. My breath left my body in a whoosh and I ran my fingers between his pecs, then scraped a nipple with my fingertip. "Holy shit," I breathed out. "I've only seen a body like yours in anatomy books."

"Makes sense. I modeled for them."

I couldn't stop a chuckle as I met his eyes. "How old are you?"

"Thirty-two. Next month."

I swallowed. Well, it was more of a gulp. "Shit."

"What's wrong?"

I shook my head. "Nothing. It's all good."

Except you're about to fuck an old lady.

But, no biggie. I'd only been with three men in my life, all of whom were older than me, and one had just become my ex-husband. But Clutch was a child. Four years younger than me. Jesus. I hoped he didn't notice all the squishy bits on my rapidly-approaching-forty body.

"Babe, I know I came in hard, but if you wanna stop, we stop."

"No, it's good. I'm just trying to take it all in. It's been a while for me."

"You really divorced?" he asked. "I don't break up families."

"Sadly, we were never a family. And, yes, we're really divorced."

His hand slid to my neck and he leaned close, nose-to-nose. "You sure you want to do this?"

"Yes. But just tonight, okay?"

"Yeah, baby. Just tonight," he whispered, kissing me again.

I wrapped my arms around his waist and flattened my palms against his muscular back as I tried to memorize every sinewy ridge and dip. This was gonna need to last me for a while.

His hands went to my jeans and he unzipped them, pushing them down my hips, panties and all, before lifting me again and setting me on the bed. "Lie back, honey."

I did, raising my knees as he removed the rest of his clothes (but kept his boxer briefs on), and hovered above me. "We're gonna take our time, okay?"

I nodded. "My, um, vibrators are in the front pocket of my overnight bag," I said motioning to the luggage on the floor.

"What for?"

"To bring me home, so to speak."

He frowned. "I don't need a vibrator to bring you home, baby."

"Pretty sure you do."

He sat up on his knees. "Come again?"

"It's nothing to be embarrassed about," I rushed to say. "A lot of women can't achieve orgasm without some form of assistance."

He cocked his head, his expression one of true confusion. "Are you telling me you've never had an orgasm?"

"No, I'm not telling you that."

"Gina, have you ever had an orgasm without a vibrator?"

"No."

"Your husband…?"

I covered my face with my hands. "Can we please not bring him into this bed? I bought a new one, so I could forget about him."

My hands were tugged away, and Clutch was once again over me. "You won't need a vibrator, baby. I'm gonna take care of you, and we're not goin' anywhere until you fuckin' come all over your sheets."

I snorted. "Good luck, buddy."

"And don't try to fake it," he demanded. "I'll know."

"Fine," I breathed out, dropping my arms back onto my duvet. "Have at it."

* * *

Clutch

She looked so fuckin' vulnerable staring up at me in disbelief. I couldn't believe not one man had taken the time to worship her body the way it deserved to be worshiped. That stopped now. I leaned over her and traced her collarbone with my lips, my tongue swirling one nipple, then the other. Her breath came out in tiny pants as her tits heaved against my mouth.

I cupped one in my hand, and sucked a nipple into my mouth, gently biting down as she whimpered beneath me.

"Gorgeous, baby," I whispered, blowing on the skin I'd just soaked with my tongue.

Her nipple tightened in the cool air, and her fingernails dug into my back as she arched against me, but when I slid my hand between her legs, she let out a quiet mew, opening her legs further.

I slid my finger inside of her, deeper into her soft heat.

"Clutch," she said on a whimper, as her hands gripped my shoulders. She was already soaked, and I'd barely touched her.

Vibrator, my ass.

Dipping lower, I ran my finger through her slick heat, spreading it on her clit as I rolled her hard nub under my fingertip.

She let out a quiet squeak as I added pressure to her clit, and another finger between her folds. Gina's hips ground down against my hand, her tits heaving with the motion, and I couldn't stop myself from reaching up and cupping one in my free hand.

"What do you want, baby?"

"More."

"More of what?"

"That!"

I pinched her clit between my thumb and finger while I

rolled her nipple with my other hand. "More of this?"

"God, yes."

Pulling away from her, I pushed my boxers down my body and settled on my knees, between her legs, kissing her thighs as I spread them apart. Fuck. Her pussy was perfect. Bare and wet, and begging to be licked.

I slid my finger into her as I covered her clit with my lips, sucking gently, then adding another finger and pressing deeply until I heard her mewl again. I was learning her language. Body and otherwise, as I figured out what she liked and disliked.

Burying my fingers deeper inside of her, I swept them against her walls as I searched for her hidden gem and tried not to come at the sight of her thrashing against the mattress. She was so fucking beautiful in the throes of ecstasy, and I wasn't sure how long I would last.

I fisted my cock to try and stop the inevitable, but when her walls began to contract against my fingers, I knew I couldn't wait. I grabbed a condom, slid it on, then thrust my cock deep inside of her.

Fuckin' heaven.

I took a second to enjoy the feeling of her tight walls surrounding me, then I buried myself deeper and deeper, slamming into her until I felt her fingernails dig into my biceps.

"What do you want, baby?" I demanded as I thrust harder into her.

"More!" she begged.

"Don't come, Gina."

"I—"

"Don't fuckin' come," I said again, and slid my hand between us to finger her clit.

"Clutch!" she screamed as her body exploded around my cock, soaking me as I gave one last thrust and joined her in ecstasy.

Holding her tight, I rolled us so we were facing each

other, and kissed her. I gently wiped the tears from her cheeks and lifted her chin. "Hey. Did I hurt you?"

She pressed her lips into a thin line and shook her head.

"You sure?"

She laid her hand over my mouth and nodded. "Shh. I'm *feeling*."

I grinned, kissing her fingers. "You feel, baby, I'm gonna get rid of this condom."

Gina grabbed my arm. "You're going to wait a minute."

"Hmm, bossy, I like it."

She licked her lips and leaned forward to kiss me again. "You made me come."

"Told you I would."

She rolled her eyes. "Forgive me for not believing you. Obviously, I've never heard that before."

I laughed. "Yeah, but I don't lie."

She sighed. "Not about that, no."

"You gonna let me clean up now?"

"Yes. But don't be long. I want to do that again."

I slid out of her and kissed her. "We've got all night, beautiful. By the morning, you won't be able to walk straight."

"I'm counting on that, handsome."

SIX

BURNING SAINTS

Clutch

I WOKE UP to the sound of slamming cupboard doors, grinding beans, and clinking glasses. I had no idea what time it was, but it felt early. Really fucking early. I was naked as a jay bird and could smell a heavenly mixture of Eldie's sweet scent on the empty sheets beside me, and freshly brewed coffee. I called out for her but got no reply, so I threw my jeans on and went to the kitchen to investigate. On my way out of the bedroom, I caught sight of the alarm clock on the nightstand; it read 5:13am.

"Oh, good, you're awake," Eldie said with about three hundred fucking percent too much cheer in her voice. She was wearing an oversized T-shirt that hung down low, exposing her shoulders. She wore nothing else, except perhaps panties, but the shirt hung too low for me to see. I desperately wanted to rectify that problem.

"I'm so glad you're an early riser, too."

"I don't even know what those words mean," I growled.

"Oh, sorry. Did I wake you?" she asked sheepishly.

"Well it was either you or some meth-head barista that was running through your kitchen."

"I was looking for tea and decaf just in case you preferred either of those," she said.

"Again, Doc. Those words mean nothing too me."

"Regular coffee it is then," she said, smiling.

"Black please, and a beer if you've got one."

"Coffee and beer?" She raised an eyebrow.

"Nothing like a good ol' Portland speedball for breakfast to cure a hangover," I replied. "Two sips of coffee, one sip of beer. Repeat until the world stops spinning enough to get on your bike and ride again."

"Riding out so early?" Eldie asked.

"Well, I figured you'd prefer me gone sooner than later, thus the early wake up call."

"Oh, god no. I'm so sorry. I wasn't trying to roust you. I've always had a hard time sleeping in. I guess I'm so used to living alone now that I didn't realize how much noise I was making. Please feel free to stay as long as you'd like. I can make you breakfast. I'd be happy to whip you up some eggs, or bacon, or whatever."

"Doc, it's okay," I said, putting my hand on her bare shoulders. "Relax, just sit down and have some coffee with me. Honestly, after last night I'm surprised you're on two feet right now."

Eldie twisted up her face in a way that made her look like a little girl who'd just taken a swig of cough syrup.

"To be honest with you I feel like Charlene ran me over in the middle of the night."

I almost spit my coffee out. "Goddammit, Doc, you've

gotta warn me before you say funny shit like that, unless you want to have to remodel your beautiful kitchen."

"You think I'm funny?" she asked, her face now glowing.

"Funny, sexy, smart, great in bed. The whole package."

"Yeah, about that," she said looking down at her cup.

"I know, Doc. This was a one-night thing. I heard you loud and clear, and we need not say a word about this, or repeat it ever again," I said, giving her the "scout's honor" salute before taking another sip of coffee.

"What if I want to repeat it?"

I'd picked a bad time to sip.

"Jesus, Doc. I'm tellin' you, you've gotta stop doin' that," I said wiping coffee from my beard with my hand.

"Let me get you a towel," she said.

"It's okay. I've gotta go," I said, standing.

"You've got to go? It's not even five-thirty in the morning. You were dead asleep five minutes ago. Where do you have to go?"

"Look, it's a great thing you woke me up early. I should really get back to the Sanctuary, and to the picnic before Minus notices I'm gone," I said, setting the coffee cup on the table.

"Minus needs to know where you are at all times?"

"It's more like I don't want him to know where I am currently. Like I said Doc, Minus told me straight up. You are off limits."

"Off limits? Who's limits? Who the hell is Minus to decide who I can and cannot sleep with?" She snapped.

"It's not like that. It's about who *I* can and cannot sleep with, and you are on that list."

"There's a list?" She asked, her voice now with an edge to it. "How many women are on this list of women that Minus has to order you to stay away from?"

"It's not like that."

"What's it like then?" she asked, folding her arms. "You don't know this about me, and maybe it'll be hard for you to believe after the way I acted last night, but I'm normally a very guarded and reserved person, and it took more than you could ever know for me to have a one-night stand with anyone, let alone a...biker, no offense."

"Some taken," I said, but motioned for her to continue.

"Well, it took a lot for me to do something like that last night, and it took a lot for me to admit that I want it to happen again, and you'll have to forgive me if it hurts my feelings to be shot down in flames by my first...booty call."

"I don't see you as a booty call. Doc, I think you're amazing, and last night was incredible. Would I love for it to happen again? Of course, I would. But the truth is, it shouldn't have happened in the first place because my club's president told me not to touch you. Do you under-stand?"

"No, Clutch. I don't understand your club's culture code or whatever."

"You make us sound like a shitty eighties band or something," I joked.

"Don't make me laugh, I'm trying to be serious here. Last night you made me feel in ways I've never felt be-fore, and I want to feel that way again. I want *you* to make me feel that way again, Clutch. I *need* you to make me feel that way again."

Eldie looked at me with a lustful fire in her eyes like I'd never seen before in any woman. I was compelled to do as she asked. Driven to fulfill her every desire. To push her to the brink of ecstasy. Even though I knew Minus would kill me for disobeying him, I had to let Gina Gard-ner know that last night was only the beginning of where I could take her.

"Now," she whispered.

"I'm out of condoms, we used them all last night."

* * *

Gina

Damn! If I'd been prepared, I'd have a couple of boxes lying around for just this situation, but up until last night, I'd had no idea any of this would happen.

"I'm on the pill," I said, and imagined myself trying to reel the words back in.

"That's not the only reason to use rubbers, Gina."

I rolled my eyes. "Cute, Clutch. Are you clean?"

"Yeah, I'm clean. I don't fuck ungloved, but regardless, I get tested regularly."

I bit my lip. "Then I'd like to be your first."

A low growl sounded in his throat and he lifted me onto the kitchen island, stepping between my legs. "You sure?"

I nodded. "But then we can stop."

"How many do you want before we stop?"

"How many what?"

"Orgasms."

I widened my eyes. "How many can you give me?"

He glanced over my shoulder. "I need to get out of here before nine. Gives us about three hours. I can give you at least ten."

I shuddered. "How about twelve?"

"I can do that." He slipped a hand between my legs and fingered my clit. "Spread, Gina."

I spread, scooting my butt closer to the edge while leaning back on my hands. He guided my legs over his shoulders and his mouth covered my core while his fingers worked my clit and I thought I'd cry with the beauty of it all.

I had never felt like this. Ever. He played my body like a violin, and I wanted the symphony to go on forever.

His fingers swept my walls and I dug my heels into his back as he sucked harder on my clit. He added a finger and I dropped my head with a moan. "Clutch," I rasped.

"Get there, baby."

I bit my lip. "I don't want to."

He chuckled. "You want twelve, right?"

I was determined to make this last, but when his thumb pressed against my super sensitive nub, I could no longer wait, exploding around his fingers.

He removed his hand, kissed my clit, then sucked his fingers dry. "Honey, baby."

I smiled, letting the post-climax glow settle into my soul.

"Don't get comfortable," he warned, helping me off the island and tugging my shirt off. "After I'm done with you, you're gonna fall into bed and sleep for hours."

I smiled, kissing him. "Looking forward to it."

Turning me away from him, one hand went to my throat, while the other cupped my mound. "I love your neck," he whispered as he bent me over my kitchen island and pushed gently on my back. "Tits to the marble, Gina."

"Ohmigod," I breathed out, the cold against my nipples, the feeling so amazing, I almost came right then and there, but then Clutch slid into me from behind, and I lost my mind.

"Hold on, baby," he warned.

I gripped the edge of the island while he pounded into me so hard an orgasm washed over me faster than expected, and I screamed his name as I came. He thrust one more time, then I felt his cock pulse inside of me as he let out a grunt and settled his palm on my lower back. "Fuckin' perfect."

I smiled. "Yes."

"You good?"

"I'm so good."

He slid gently out of me and I pushed away from the counter, wrapping my arms around his neck. "That's two."

Clutch grinned, lifting me so I could wrap my legs

around him. "Where to?"

"Bedroom."

He kissed me again, then carried me down the hall and into my room, dropping me onto the mattress. "You ready?"

I nodded, and he settled his hand on my belly. "On your knees."

"Don't you need a minute?"

He glanced down. "Does it look like I need a minute?"

My gaze drifted down to his already hard penis. No, it certainly did not.

I flipped onto my knees, then got on all-fours, and he slid into me from behind without warning. I wanted more.

Clutch's palm connected with my ass and I thought I'd come right there and then. Another slap and I whimpered, pushing my body back against him.

"Had a feelin' you'd like that," he rasped, and slammed into me again, his palm slapping me a little harder this time and the sensation overtook everything.

"Fuck!" I breathed out. "Yes!"

"Don't move," he ordered, and slid out of me.

"What the hell are you doing?" I growled.

He pulled open my toy drawer, then settled himself behind me again.

"Clutch," I hissed.

He chuckled. "Trust me, baby."

I threw my head back, my long hair sweeping my back, which Clutch wrapped in his fist, tugging gently. "You gonna stow the attitude?"

"You gonna make me come?" I returned.

He swept something between my legs, then his cock was inside me again and I sighed with pleasure. Except, it wasn't pleasure.

What came next was pleasure.

In the form of a vibrator pressing into my very private area.

"Clutch," I said on a whimper.

Then he moved. Holy shit, the man moved.

He buried his cock deep inside of me, then matched the motion of the vibrator with his hips. I screamed as an orgasm swamped me and I cried out his name again.

His body locked, and he wrapped his arms around me, gently rolling us to the side so we were spooning, staying connected as he kissed the back of my neck. "God damn, baby. Fuckin' sexy as hell."

"I like what you did with that vibrator," I admitted.

"I know. I was here."

I chuckled. "Brat."

His hand slid between my legs and cupped my mound. "Hook your leg over mine."

With his dick still inside of me, I slid my leg over his thigh and he slapped my pussy. I jumped a little, but he held me tighter, pressing his hand against my clit and pushing my core back against him.

"Good?"

I licked my lips and nodded.

He slapped my pussy again and I pressed back against him, drawing his cock in deeper.

"You're fuckin' soaked," he whispered, slapping me again.

"Believe me when I say this has never happened before."

His fingers pressed against my clit as he chuckled. "Glad I could be of service."

I seriously didn't think one more day was going to be enough, but we'd made a deal and I always kept my deals.

He slapped my pussy again and I could no longer think coherently. So, I didn't. I just felt. I needed these memories to pull from in the future, and at the rate he was going, I was going to have a lot to use.

Clutch

"**S**HIT, I REALLY *do* have to get out of here," I said, looking at my watch.

"I feel like I've heard this song before," Eldie said smiling up at me.

"Yeah, but this time I mean it. The picnic is an all-hands kind of deal, and if Minus counts me as AWOL, he'll chew my ass twice as hard as anyone else."

"Why's that?" she asked.

"Lots of reasons, I guess. Because he's my best friend, mostly. Then, because I'm the club's Sergeant, but then it's just because Minus likes to bust my balls whenever he can."

"Why are guys like that?"

"It's not just a guy thing. Minus and me are more like brothers," I explained.

"I didn't realize you two were so close. By the time the Saints started requesting me by name at the ER, Minus had moved away, so I never saw much of him," Eldie said, running her fingers over my chest. "Are you some sort of gym rat?"

"Not exactly, but I do try to stay in good shape and at fighting weight even when I'm not in training."

"Training?" she asked.

"For a fight. I compete in boxing matches from time to time."

"Is that something you do professionally?"

"Amateur bouts. I don't care about the money. I just like fighting. Imposing my will on the other fighter. Seeing the look in his eye when he knows I've beaten him. That's all good. Sometimes I even like getting hit in the face myself." I laughed.

"How could that be fun?"

"I didn't say it was fun. More like useful."

"How so?"

"Getting smacked in the chops reminds you that you're alive. Reminds you that this whole life is one big fist fight. Every day is capable of delivering a clean hit to the chin and it's only how you stand up to that blow that matters. Then, if you can withstand the blows that life throws at you, one day, it becomes your time to hit back."

Eldie shifted a bit in my arms.

"I don't understand all the need for fighting," she said.

"You don't always have a choice. Fighting is built into some people, and some are molded into fighters through circumstances," I said.

"Which is true for you?" she asked.

"Both, I guess."

"Well, if you have to fight, I hope you find something worth fighting for someday," she said before quickly changing the subject.

"Are you naturally this hairless?" she asked.

"No way."

"But, you're so smooth," she murmured. "Do you shave?"

"Gotta wax that shit, baby, or I couldn't contain it."

She chuckled. "Why not?"

"I'm Greek," I said.

"Ah, thus the last name I can't seem to remember or pronounce," she said.

"Christakos," I replied.

"At first I thought you were giving that officer an alias."

I laughed. "Nikolai Christakos, but my close friends call me Nicky."

"Am I your friend?" she asked, looking up at me with her doe eyes. It took every ounce of my will power not to roll on top of her for another round right then and there.

"I think it's safe to say that what we've been doing for the past twelve hours puts us somewhere past friends," I said. "But don't worry, Doc, I know this was a one time, or two time, as it were, deal. I'll get outta your hair and back to the Sanctuary." I gently rolled her off my chest and sat at the edge of the bed.

"I could come with you," Eldie said, cheerfully.

"It's okay, Doc, I'll check in with Mayday about your car and let you know as soon as it's ready."

"That's not what I meant," she said, placing her hands on my chest from behind.

"I don't think that would be a good idea," I said standing quickly.

"And why is that?" she asked, still topless, her arms folded, one eyebrow raised.

"Come on, Doc, it's not even fuckin' fair," I said, exasperated.

"What's the problem, *Nicky*?"

I felt the blood drain from my head. In fact, it felt as though every drop of blood rushed to one area, my dick. When Eldie said my name, I wanted to tell Minus and the whole world to take their rules and shove them up their asses. If only life was that simple, but I damned well knew it wasn't. Within that was the knowledge that Dr. Gina Gardner was by no means meant for any kind of life alongside a dirtbag biker with no future.

"You're the problem, Doc," I said.

"Me?"

"You're the sexiest, most beautiful woman I've ever seen in my life, and I've had an amazing time. Thank you, I have to go," I said picking up a boot from the floor. "Have you seen my other boot?"

"That's it?" she exclaimed.

"Look, Doc, I know you were married for a while, and maybe you're new to the whole one-night stand thing, but this is kind of how they work. You get drunk, you fuck, and then you split in the morning before things get awkward."

"Whoa, so now this was just an awkward drunken fuck?" Eldie was no longer smiling.

"Nope, not what I said or meant." I sat back down on the bed and put my hands on her shoulders. The feel of her smooth skin felt amazing under my rough, scarred hands. "I meant what I said, I think you are just about the perfect woman, but this can't happen again."

"Just about perfect? What does that mean?" she asked.

"The only thing that isn't perfect is that you're unavailable."

"Excuse me? I'm fairly sure I've made myself available to you last night, *and this morning.*"

"That's not what I mean. Minus said that you're off limits to me, so the only story he's ever gonna hear is that I dropped you off at your place and then went home. If he sees us together today, that'll be that."

"Okay, your place it is, then," Eldie said, smiling once again.

"What?"

"Look, Clutch, I'm not asking to be your girlfriend or anything. I just had a lot of fun blowing off steam with you last night and I'm supposed to be on vacation this weekend. I don't want to be here at my place, and my other plans are in the crapper, so, like you said, we'll go back to your place."

"Not even fuckin' fair."

* * *

Gina

Clutch stood there wearing only his jeans, one boot, and an expression of pure bewilderment on his face.

"Alright, Doc. You win. You can hang out at my place, but I really do have to get back to the picnic once I drop you off."

"Fair enough, but I want to have dinner with you tonight." I couldn't believe my own ears. Who the hell was I? I'm usually the wallflower at a dinner party, begging not to be noticed or talked to. But one minor traffic collision later, and I'm a braless, sex maniac who bosses bikers into letting her crash at their pads.

Maybe I have a concussion!

"Whatever you say, Doc, but I'm warning you, my place is not the Four Seasons, and the maid has been on vacation for the past... three years, so I highly doubt you'll be comfortable there."

"I'm sure I've crashed out in worse places at the hospital back in the day," I said.

"You might need to go to the hospital if you're exposed to my place for too long," he said.

We got dressed quickly and I threw a few things in a bag, then we hit the road as the sun was greeting the day. Amidst the bizarre chaos of the past twenty-four hours, I was struck by how unusually calm I was inside. Outside of my work, my life was full of second guesses and feelings of being frozen in a lake of indecision. Professionally, I knew my place in the world, and I absolutely loved being a doctor. It brought a sense of purpose and order to my life, and I loved to serve others. I was more than happy doing anything that pulled focus away from me.

Clutch rode us up to a little ranch house in North Portland and I was surprised by how cute it was, at least from the outside.

He unlocked his door and stepped aside so I could walk in. He wasn't wrong. The house needed a good cleaning…at least it didn't smell. Clothes lay strewn about in seemingly random places, next to stacks of boxes and motorcycle parts.

"I warned you," Clutch grumbled, closing us into his small foyer.

"Did I say anything?"

"I could hear your disdain."

I raised an eyebrow. "Neat trick. Have you thought of taking it on the road? Or maybe a residency in Vegas?"

His hand went to my neck and he kissed me. "Now I hear your pussy beggin' for more."

I rolled my eyes.

"But I gotta go."

I raised my hands in surrender. "I'm not stopping you."

He kissed me again. "Would you stop gabbin'?" he demanded. "The guilt trip isn't gonna work."

I couldn't stop a snort as I forced back a laugh. "Go!"

"Is this reverse psychology? 'Cause that ain't gonna work either."

"Oh my God, Nicky, get your ass out of here."

He kissed me one more time and walked out the door. I turned to face the tiny formal living room and sighed. There was no way in hell I could hang out here all day and not tidy up...*just* a little bit.

* * *

Clutch

This was by far the strangest one night stand I'd ever had. I was simply gonna follow Doc's lead, because I had no fucking idea what was going on here. Clearly, we had sexual chemistry together, but there was no possible way this, whatever it was, could go on much longer. I'm not sure what it was that allowed her to put so much trust in me, but it scared the shit outta me. She had no idea what kind of monster I was, and I wanted to keep it that way. I knew I was gonna need to cut her loose ASAP, but I didn't want her to run away from me screaming. Even though we could share a laugh and a bed, there was no way we could share any kind of life together, and I knew it. She was a doctor, for fuck's sake. She'd dedicated her life to saving the very dirtbags that I'd put in the hospital. Her colleagues down in the morgue were putting toe tags on guys that I'd iced.

I pulled up to the Sanctuary to find the picnic in progress. I wouldn't say it was in full swing, but half swing, at least. Saints and their lady friends were laid out on every couch, chair, and available mattress. Some brothers were still up from the night before, and others were just waking up to drink their breakfasts. Every bin was already overflowing with beer cans and food containers, and the weekend wasn't even over. An empty bulk box of condoms lay next to a stack of pizza boxes. As bad as my place was, I was glad Eldie was there and not here. Ropes spotted me and gave me a chin lift.

"Hey, Brother. Minus was looking for you earlier. He's out back playing horseshoes," he said as he walked by, before disappearing into the kitchen.

I raised a hand in acknowledgement and headed over to the garage. Before anything, I wanted to make sure that

Eldie's Jeep was being taken care of, but when I got there, I found all the lights off, and no sign of Mayday, or any of his crew. Irritated, I turned and headed for the horseshoe pits.

I spotted Minus in the distance, standing with a group of Saints near the horseshoe pits. He was sipping a cup of coffee, smiling, looking like a man without a fuckin' care in the world. I didn't know how he did it. How he was able to carry the weight of other people's burdens, and yet appear light as a feather. I didn't have a third of the responsibilities that he had, and I felt like I was barely holding my shit together half of the time.

"Hey, Clutch, where you been hidin'?" Minus said as I approached.

"I've been around," I said, hoping his line of questioning would stop there. "Speaking of who's around, have you seen Mayday?"

"He and his crew hit it pretty hard last night, I think he's still passed out in his rack. Why?" Minus asked.

"I asked him to jump on Eldie's rig ASAP, and he told me he'd be right on it. I went by the shop, but it's a ghost town," I said.

"Of course, it's closed. Look around man, it's picnic time," Minus said smiling, his arms stretched out wide, his face to the sun.

"I told him I wanted him on it right away," I said.

"Yeah, well, right away means first thing Monday, because these guys all need and deserve some R&R, so leave Mayday the fuck alone. Besides, why do you care so much about Eldie's car?"

"Just trying to look out for the club's doctor is all," I said as innocently as possible. "And make sure Mayday's on top of things. The last few jobs I've had for him, he's dragged ass."

"I'm sure he'll take care of Eldie as soon as he's able. C'mon, throw some shoes with us," Minus said, jovially.

"Sure, sounds great. Lemme grab a beer and I'll join you," I said, pasting a smile on my face.

I've got Eldie and her fine ass walking around my place right now and I'm gonna be stuck here on sausage island all day long. I couldn't wait for the festivities of the evening to kick in again, so I could slip away unnoticed. Until then I was gonna nurse a few light beers, toss some horseshoes, and otherwise do whatever else I had to do in order to bide my time and stay under the radar.

* * *

Gina

I raided Clutch's fridge sometime around noon and found nothing edible. There was a shit ton of beer, but no protein, fruit, or vegetables, which meant, I either headed to the store, or I starved. I sighed. I couldn't believe I was stuck here with nothing to eat.

Rummaging through his drawers, I found a spare house key, confirmed it worked, then called an Uber. Time to do some grocery shopping, despite the fact he didn't have reusable bags. Lord this man was a bachelor with a capital B.

Luckily, there was a Freddie's less than a mile from his place, so I hit every aisle, from produce to cleaning supplies. He had next to nothing, so I'd had to clean the counters with Windex. Not particularly hygienic, so first item in the basket was cleaning wipes.

All-in-all, I spent close to an hour in the store. I hated shopping, but decided I'd do my own weekly stock-up while I was here. Kill a couple of birds and all that.

Once I checked out, I called for another car and headed back to Clutch's place, the steaks the size of my head, in tow. I noticed he had a really nice grill, so I decided I'd marinate the meat and he could cook it when he got home.

I let myself into Clutch's home and headed straight for the kitchen. I had to guess where he liked his groceries stocked, on account of the fact, he didn't actually *have* any groceries, so I made a few executive decisions, then went about prepping dinner.

By three p.m., I thought my head would explode from the boredom. And the worry. What the hell was I doing here? I was waiting for my boy toy to get back from 'work,' so I could have another orgasm…or six.

God! I'd become one of *those* women. You know, the kind who quickly became addicted to a man totally wrong for them only because he was good in bed? And, holy shit, Clutch was *great* in bed. So great, in fact, I wanted him right now.

I bit my lip. I should have brought one of my vibrators with me. Not the one he'd used this morning…maybe the rabbit. Shit. I needed to distract myself. Clutch didn't even have a TV. What kind of maniac doesn't own a television?

Cleaning.

I could clean.

I'd done a cursory tidy up earlier, but I had no idea what time Clutch would arrive home, which meant I had nervous energy to work out.

Cleaning it was.

I gathered up my newly purchased rubber gloves and supplies and started in his bedroom.

Wrong move.

Jealousy, the level of which I'd never experience before, reared its ugly head, and I suddenly had flashes of other women in his bed. Admittedly, this made me a little crazy as I ripped his sheets off the bed, comforter and all, and shoved everything into the washing machine, as burning it seemed a tad excessive. I was hoping we'd end up in his bed, and there was no way in hell I was going to contract some whore's STD residue left on his bedding.

While everything was washing, I attacked his bathroom. This took a little more effort. Men really were quite gross, which meant it took an entire wash cycle to make his bathroom usable.

Transferring everything to the dryer, I focused on the rest of the house. Which was surprisingly quite lovely. It was obvious someone had put some work into it. His kitchen had been updated...not in a style I could get behind, but it was perfect for a single man.

There were hand-scraped hardwood floors throughout, and his furniture was comfortable, and practical, even if it wasn't very pretty. I suppose a badass biker wouldn't be caught dead in anything 'stylish,' so it suited him.

The dryer finished its cycle just as I wrapped the cord of the vacuum around the handle, (thank the lord the man owned a vacuum), so I headed back to the bedroom to make the bed. By the time that chore was done, I heard the front door close and Clutch was calling my name.

EIGHT

BURNING SAINTS

Clutch

"**D**OC," I CALLED, after locking the front door. The smell of something clean and piney assaulted my nose as I walked into the great room. The extremely clean great room.

"Back here," she answered, and I headed for the master bedroom.

I stalled at the threshold. She was smoothing her hands over the comforter of my freshly made bed. "You cleaned?"

"I did." She blew her hair away from her face and stood up straight. "You weren't kidding about the maid being gone."

"You didn't need to do that."

"Um, well, considering you haven't met a dust bunny you didn't love, and you had no food in your fridge…" she waved a finger, "…fermented hops don't count."

I chuckled. "Yeah, I figured we'd order in."

"No, it's okay. I went shopping."

"Come again?"

"I bought a few groceries, and noticed you have a really nice grill, so I grabbed some steaks. The bakers are in the oven now, so you can grill while I do the rest."

"Are you shittin' me?"

She smiled. "Come on, I'll show you."

I followed her down the hall and into the spotless kitchen and she opened the fridge and the cabinets closest to it, fully stocked with pretty high-class shit.

"You didn't need to do this, Doc."

"Yeah, I kinda did," she said. "You had *nothing* here. Plus, I needed wine."

"Wow, this is all very…domestic," I said, and the smile dropped from Eldie's face.

"I'm sorry, I didn't mean to make you uncomfortable. I—"

"No, it's great. I didn't mean it to sound that way, it's just that I'm not used to there being a woman in my house."

"I found enough pieces of women's clothing around here to suggest otherwise, unless of course those were your panties under the bed," she teased.

"Oh, Jesus, Doc."

"It's okay, Clutch, it's not like I thought you were a virgin or anything. Besides, I'm not even here and I never was, remember?"

"That's right. But what I meant was, I'm not used to having a woman shop and clean for me," I replied.

"Who said I did this for you?" Eldie's smile lit up her face. "I did this for me, out of sheer boredom. Okay, maybe a little pity, but don't get used to it."

"Got it. Now, I'll get the grill fired up while you open that bottle of wine."

We sat in silence, seated across from each other as we ate our dinner. I couldn't recall a single time when I'd actually eaten at my kitchen table. This felt...right in a weird way.

"Penny for your thoughts?" Eldie asked, after a while.

"I'm sorry. I'm not being very good company, am I?"

"I think, 'Gee, Doc, these potatoes are amazing,' was the last thing you said, five minutes ago," she said smiling. "And, by the way, the steak is cooked to perfection."

"Probably because of your marinade."

"Are you okay?"

"Yeah, Doc. Just got a lot on my mind."

"I got a good way to distract you."

"Yeah?"

She nodded. "Unless you want dessert."

"You're dessert enough."

She chuckled. "I was kind of hoping you'd say that."

I grabbed the dishes and dumped them in the sink before wrapping my arms around her and kissing her like she deserved, then leading her down to the freshly cleaned master.

We tore at each other's clothing, leaving everything where it fell, and I pulled her close, needing to be inside of her. Once she was naked, I guided her onto the bed and wove my fingers through hers. "So fuckin' beautiful," I rasped, sliding my hand between her legs and circling her clit with my thumb as I pressed a finger inside of her.

She grabbed my arms as her head fell back and she let out the sexiest fuckin' groan that nearly made me come right then.

Her fingers dug into me. "More, Clutch."

"I'm going to make you come so hard." I swept my fingers against her G-spot.

"Holy...Jebus." Her body trembled as I rubbed her clit,

trailing my mouth down to her nipples. I bit her nipple then sucked through the sting.

"Oh my god," she cried out.

Her pussy started to contract around my finger, and I shoved a second one inside her.

"Come," I demanded.

Her legs shaking, her pussy contracting, her nipples hard as fuck, she exploded around me. "Clutch," she panted out.

Stroking her through her aftershocks, I gently pushed her back to the bed, kissing down her stomach, to the top of her pussy, I replaced my thumb with my tongue and sucked her clit, working in tight circles as her thigh muscles tightened around my head.

"I don't know how much more I can take," she whispered.

Holy fuck, she tasted like heaven. "I got you, baby." I crawled up her body, leaving a trail of kisses over every beautiful inch of her.

Grabbing my hair, she pulled my face up. "I want you inside me."

Fisting myself, I rubbed the head of my cock through her wet heat. "Your wish is my command."

She grinned and spread her legs wider as I grabbed a condom and shoved into her.

She gasped, and I stilled. "You okay?"

"So good. I just don't want this to end.

Stroking her cheek, I smiled. "Gonna make it last, baby."

"Gonna hold you to that."

My dick pulsed as I pulled out a couple inches then gently rocked into her.

"Harder," she whispered, digging her fingers into my ass and thrusting her hips up.

No holding back now, I drove into her. Hard.

"Again," she demanded.

Adrenaline spiked, and I flipped her over. "On your knees," I ordered.

Going on all fours, she raised her sweet ass in the air and threw her head back. I grabbed her hair and twisted it around my hand. "Not even fuckin' fair," I breathed, running a hand over her ass.

"You gonna make this good for me?" she challenged.

"You doubtin' me right now?" I returned, driving into her as I dragged my lips and my teeth up her spine.

She didn't respond, so I gave her a firm, quick smack. "You gonna answer me, Gina?"

"You gonna keep doing that?" she retorted.

I pulled back then shoved in deep and fast. "What do you want, baby?"

"I want you to fuck me harder."

I leaned over her, gripping her chin and turning her head. "Harder?"

"Yes, Clutch, harder."

I fucked her harder until her pussy contracted around my cock, then I let myself go. For the rest of the night, we alternated between dessert and sex. Occasionally dessert *on* her sex, which was my personal favorite.

By the time we fell into oblivion, I was out of rubbers and her pussy had been well satisfied. For the first night ever, I let a woman stay. In my bed. And I held said woman all night long.

Clutch

THE NEXT MORNING, I opened my front door just wide enough for Minus to see me and hoped Eldie was well out of sight.

"Hey man, what's goin' on?" Minus greeted me.

"Nothin', just uh, hangin' out," I said, trying to act casually, but apparently not well enough.

"What the fuck's goin' on in there?

"Nothin'."

"You keepin' a lady friend company, Nicky?" Minus asked, craning his neck for a better peek inside. I slinked outside, closing the door behind me.

"Oh, shit you do. Sorry man," Minus said, smiling.

"No worries, man, what's up?" I asked.

"What are you bein' so cagey about, brother? Who do you have in there? Is it someone I know?"

"I dunno, maybe, I don't think so," I replied nervously.

"Holy shit! Is it that new waitress at Sally Anne's? I thought I saw her at the picnic. The redhead with the big—"

"Yeah, man. Anyway, what's goin' on? You said you needed me for some business," I said trying to steer Minus away from my sex life.

"Kitty's back in town," he said.

"No shit," I said, and let out a long whistle.

"Yup."

"Do the Dogs know?" I asked.

"Crow called me directly," he replied.

"Shit, the Prez himself? Why not your buddy Hatch?" I asked dryly. Hatch was Cricket's brother, and the Dogs of Fire's Sergeant at Arms. To say that he and Minus didn't always see eye to eye would be an understatement.

"It's because of Hatch that Crow reached out. It seems as though Hatch got himself pinched by the feds and Kitty has the intel they need to clear his name. Local PD is currently holding him until the FBI can pick him up, and they need our help getting him out."

"Holy shit."

"Yup, and that ain't even the half of it. It was our pals Los Psychos that paid Kitty to help frame Hatch. Crow is calling in his favor and needs us to get some sort of code key from Kitty, *whatever it takes*."

I looked at Minus. "You okay with us getting our hands dirty?"

"I don't have a choice. Besides, I'm hoping Kitty wants money more than he wants blood."

"Let's hope so, because that guy is eight feet of angry fucking nerd, and it's gonna take a crew of us to get him into a van," I said.

"Let's just hope it doesn't come to that. When Kitty left town, he was still on good terms with the Saints. Hopefully, he still sees our colors as friendly."

"Jesus, an ex-Dog and Los Psychos working together. Why not come after us? We're the ones that fucked up Los Psychos' Portland operation."

"Yeah, with help from Hatch and the Dogs of Fire," Minus said. "And just because we're hearing about this attack on the Dogs first, it doesn't mean they haven't executed some sort of attack on us already."

"We need to get to Kitty, fast. If Los Psychos are coming after us, we need to know about it sooner than later," I said.

"Alright, grab your kit and kiss the waitress goodbye," Minus said.

"She's not—"

"Oh, and bring the zap rods too will ya," Minus said, walking away. I went back inside and called out.

"Doc," I whisper shouted. "Doc, you can come out now."

No reply.

"Eldie, the coast is clear."

Nothing.

I went into the bedroom to find my back slider slightly open, and Eldie's bag gone. She must have slipped out the back while Minus and I were talking. I peeked outside, but she must have hoofed it out of there.

I headed to my bedroom and put on my boots and kutte before opening my closet door. I pulled up the carpet on the closet floor to reveal my safe's keypad. I punched in the code and retrieved my kit; a black canvas backpack that contained common tools I needed for most of the criminal enterprises I specialized in; a multi-tool, a Blackhawk QCD combat knife, a 9mm pistol with a boot holster, brass knuckles, a mini butane torch, cable ties, and a roll of duct tape. I also grabbed the duffel bag which contained a half-dozen tactical baton stun sticks. I locked up the house and left with Minus, glancing around for Eldie, but she was gone, as was any trace of her.

"Alright, so it's just the two of us then?" I asked as we got on our bikes.

Minus laughed. "The two of us against Kitty? Never in a million fuckin' years, buddy, but I love your enthusiasm. Maybe back in the day."

"Fuck that. I wouldn't bet against us today. I'm still good to go Minus, you just give me the word and I'll set it off." I could feel my muscles starting to tighten and swell. The back of my neck began to burn with the familiar adrenaline surge of marching into battle.

"Alright, brother. Just stay frosty until I say otherwise," Minus said. "I also called Ropes, the Peckers, and Wolf. They're meetin' us at Sally Anne's before we head over to Kitty's place."

Kitty, despite his cuddly name, was no fucking joke. He'd been kicked out of the Dogs of Fire years ago for being too aggressive, and at six feet seven inches, and over three hundred pounds, if he was having a bad day, he could put you in the hospital just by accident. It was no surprise why the Dogs, a clean club, wouldn't want to try and deal with Kitty without violence being on the table. Kitty was not only big and mean, but he was smart as hell. He was a national chess champion as a kid and built his first computer at nine years old. He also loved meth, PCP, and punching people hard enough to rupture their internal organs.

We pulled around the back of Sally Anne's and made our way to the side entrance before Minus stopped me.

"Hey, I meant what I said earlier. It's nice to see a bit of the old you comin' back," he said.

"What do you mean?"

"You've been moping around for over a week. You barely say jack shit to anyone, especially me."

"What the fuck do you want me to say?

"Hey man, I was only—"

"Only what? Checking up on me? Do you want a status report on my business proposal? I have it, by the way; the business proposal that you forced me to come up with and then never asked for again."

"Is that what this is about? Why you've been in such a shitty mood? Because I didn't get around to hearing your proposal at Church? I was kind of busy trying to prevent Wolf from leading an all-out insurrection if you don't recall," Minus snapped. "So, forgive me, princess, if you didn't get enough attention at the tea party."

"Fuck you, Jase. I never asked to be a member of the young entrepreneurs of America. I used to run with a fucking biker club, and now I'm supposed to turn in my kutte for a fucking smock."

"Et tu, Brute?"

"Spare me your college boy bullshit for once, you sanctimonious prick."

"Seriously, Nicky. I expected this shit from Wolf, Elwood, and some of the others, but I thought you'd have my back."

Minus truly looked shocked. I felt a little bad about that, but I was mad as hell, and this conversation had been a long time coming.

"Why? Why the fuck would I have your back when you're gonna run this club, and everything we've built within it, right into the fucking ground?"

Minus balled up his fists at his side and took a deep breath in before exhaling slowly.

"I wasn't trying to pick a fight with you Nicky. I know you're pissed at me, and there's not much I can do about that now other than to say I'm sorry, but right now I need you to trust me, and trust that I have the club's best interest at heart."

"None of that matters," I said. "Your good intentions

are gonna get us all killed. Our enemies already smell blood in the water. Today it's Los Psychos, tomorrow it could be the Apex Predators. Who the fuck knows? One thing is for sure, Minus. With the Burning Saints out of the ground and pound game, a vacuum has been created, and there's gonna be a lot of scary dudes lookin' to fill it."

"You don't think I'm aware of that, or that Cutter wasn't when he set this whole thing in motion? Don't forget, Nicky, it was your mentor that came up with the plan to turn the Saints legit."

"Not that he ever said shit to me about it," I snapped.

"There it is. *There it fucking is,*" Minus said.

"Please, oh wise one. Fill me in on what you *think* you know."

"You're jealous. Since day one you've been pissed that Cutter named me as President and not you," he said.

"Yep, that's it, Minus. You're a fucking genius and a great leader. Now, can we go inside, the garbage out here stinks almost as bad as your horse shit."

"See, you try to shut me out every time I try to talk to you lately. I was only trying to say that rolling around with the waitress seemed to lighten your mood, and you start a fuckin' war with me."

"I'm not rolling—"

"I'm not finished," Minus said. "I don't give a shit if you're pissed at me, or jealous, or just on your fucking period, I need you focused and onboard. And, on a personal note, I'd like my fuckin' best friend back."

I could see that Minus was making a genuine attempt to work out the shit between us, but I was pissed and still needed time to figure out how I felt about being in a straight-edge club, and if I had the ability to show my throat to a guy that's always been an equal to me.

"Look, Jase, I'm man enough to admit that I've been jealous of you over stupid shit throughout the years, but this ain't that. I'm not pissed that I'm not President. I told you and Cutter that I never wanted the patch, and that it could go to Warthog for all I fuckin' care."

"Then, what is it?"

"What the fuck does it matter to you what I'm thinking?" I snapped.

"You're my brother, Nicky. Of course, I care about you."

"Brother? Are you? Cutter was supposed to be a father to me, and you're supposed to be my brother; and yet neither one of you asked for my advice while you were busy planning the club's future. Shit, I've had to find out most of my news second hand, along with all the other foot soldiers. I'm the fucking Sergeant at Arms, and your best friend, and I barely know jack shit about what's gone down over the past months. And now you come at *me* for shutting *you* out? I always knew you had balls, Minus, but I never knew how big they were."

"Did you pay attention during any of our classes?" Jase asked, handing the wrench I'd just given him back to me.

"What?"

"We had all the same classes, taught by the same priests and sisters, and yet you still don't know the difference between nine sixteenths and five eights."

"Goddamned metric system," I grumbled as I rummaged through the toolbox for the correct wrench.

"What's the metric system got to do with anything? Those wrenches are standard sizes. You know what? Never mind," Jase said, rising to his feet. "If you put everything back where it belonged, you wouldn't have such a hard time finding things," he chided, before spouting out his favorite phrase, "A place for everything, and everything in—"

"Your ass!" I shouted.

Jase scowled. "Tell you what. I'll get the wrench and

you get the last two beers and the leftover Chinese from the fridge."

"Bad news, comrade, I polished off the rest of that while you were out."

Jase raised one eyebrow. His signature move. "I sure hope you mean the Chinese food and not the beer."

"I mean both," I said.

"Goddamnit, Nicky."

"I was hungry, thirsty, and...and you weren't here," I argued.

"I wasn't here because I was out looking for work all day. You know, so we can pay rent."

"Don't worry. This dump is bound to collapse before the next rent check is due."

Our home was a small commercial space that Jase and I had converted into an apartment/shop. The rent was low, but our source of income was lower. I wasn't sure if Portland was in the middle of a hiring freeze or if they were simply freezing out the likes of Jase and me. Luckily, we'd been getting a slow but steady stream of business fixing up vintage bikes via Craigslist. For young guys, Jase and I were obsessed with vintage Harleys, Indians, and Triumphs. Motorcycle manuals and parts catalogues were just about the only reading I could stomach. Unlike Jase, who I think was disappointed when we left school. You'd never know it by looking at the guy, but he was the smartest guy I knew. Hell, in our whole school. Including the priests and nuns.

Having found the correct wrench, Jase turned his attention back to the bike. "I'm not kidding, man. Were gonna run out of money soon if we don't find some serious work."

Little did Jase know, serious work was about to find us.

I was about to offer to make a beer run but was interrupted by the unmistakable sound of pipes. Not just any pipes either. *These were loud. And by loud, I mean "fuck you" loud. There were at least two bikes, and they were quickly approaching our shop.*

"You expecting someone?" Jase asked.

"Nope."

We heard bike's engines cut off, followed by footsteps and three loud bangs on the shop door.

"Who the fuck is that?" Jase said, grabbing the baseball bat we kept by the sofa-sleeper.

"How the hell should I know?" I went to the workbench, opened the bottom drawer and took out a rusty metal box. It originally served as a case for an electric drill, but it now housed a different piece of hardware. I opened the box, pulled out the .38 special inside and walked to the door.

"Where the fuck did you get a gun?"

"Where people get guns," I replied.

"How do you know where people get guns?"

"You got your education and I got mine," I said before turning my attention to our mystery guests. "Who the fuck is there?" I shouted through the metal fire door.

"The Burning Saints MC. How 'bout you open the door?" a gruff voice answered.

"How about you tell me what the fuck you want first?" I countered.

"Jesus, Nicky," Jase hissed. "Those guys are gangsters."

"I don't give a shit who they are. If they try anything with me, I'll shoot 'em right in the Chevy Chase," I replied.

"Okay, Guy Ritchie, calm the fuck down."

The voice on the other side of the door answered back. "My name's Cutter. I found you on Craigslist. I have a bike here that needs some work. You open for business?"

"How did you find us? Our address isn't on the ad."

"Look, kid. I don't like yelling at doors, so how about

you let me in and we can talk about the job."

Jase shook his head and shot me a look that said, "Don't you even think about opening that door."

"You said we need money," I reminded Jase.

"What good is money if we're dead?" he whispered.

"Nicer caskets?" I joked, then unlocked and opened the door.

Three men in full riding leathers and kuttes stood outside. Each man looked to be in his fifties and like he was not to be fucked with. I discreetly tucked the pistol in the back of my waistband.

Cutter stood front and center, his name and president's patch clearly on display. "You Jase or Nicky?" he asked.

"How do you know—?"

"May we come in?" Cutter asked. Before I could answer, he and his associates made their way inside.

"I'm Jase," my partner spoke up. "You said you had a bike for us to look at?"

"Lots of bikes, actually," Cutter replied nonchalantly, while looking around our tiny shop. "It's a place you've got here."

"Did you say, 'Nice place we've got here'?" I asked.

"No," Cutter replied.

"What can we do for you?" I asked impatiently. If this guy had work for us, I wish he'd get on with the details of the job. If he was gonna rob and murder us, he may as well get on with that as well. "What are you looking for exactly?"

"You," Cutter replied with a smile that made my blood run cold.

Jase immediately snapped into "public defender" mode. "Mr. Cutter. Whatever Nicky has said or done, I'm sure he's deeply sorry, and that we can find a way to compensate you in a satisfactory manner."

Cutter smiled. "This is Red Dog, and this is Wolf," he

said, motioning to the two men flanking him. "Red Dog heard about a couple of young guys who were fixing up old rides here in town, so I thought I'd come check out your operation. The Saints have a shop of our own and it's always nice to know who your competition is."

"Whoa," I said, putting my hands up. "We're not trying to steal business from you or anything."

"Trust me, kid. If I thought you were stealing from me, this would be an entirely different kind of conversation," Cutter said in a way that didn't make me feel any better.

"What is the nature of our...conversation?" Jase asked cautiously.

"I'm scouting for talent," he replied plainly. "I'm looking for guys who are dependable and know how to handle themselves."

"To do what, exactly?" I asked.

"Have you heard of the Burning Saints Motorcycle Club?"

"I've seen the patches around town. Heard a few stories," I said.

"Well, Nikolai. I'm not sure what you've heard about the Saints, but I've heard a few tall tales about you two. Seems like you've both already earned a bit of a reputation on the street."

If Cutter was trying to prove he'd done his homework, he could rest easy.

"What the fuck is this?" I snapped.

"I told you, it's a job interview." Cutter said.

"I don't recall either of us dropping an application off at your super-secret clubhouse," Jase said, coolly.

"That's what I've heard the most about you two."

"What's that?" I asked.

"You're not easily rattled. You stay cool under pressure and you're not afraid of getting your hands dirty. I need guys like that in my club, and you can make a shit ton more money working for me than you'll ever do as

Craigslist grease monkey."

"We're having a party tomorrow night at the Sanctuary. How 'bout you boys come hang out and see what we're all about," Red Dog said, handing me a piece of paper with an address on it.

"The Sanctuary?" I asked.

"It's our super-secret biker clubhouse," Cutter said with a wink.

"Nicky—"

Minus's voice brought me back to the present and I scowled. "Don't try to outtalk me, college boy. Look, man, the truth is you're losing this club and you're gonna lose me unless you start telling me what the fuck is going on. I think it's fair to ask that I know as much about my club's business as your girlfriend does."

"You're right," Minus said, backing up a step.

"What?" I stood stunned.

"You're absolutely right, Nicky. I've been trying to protect you and the club, but I've left you in the dark. That was not my intention, and I'm sorry."

"What the fuck is going on here?"

"I'm apologizing."

"Yeah, but…" I wasn't sure what else to say, Minus had thrown me for a loop. There were times in the past when the two of us would rather punch each other in the face than admit any kind of wrongdoing.

"The truth is exactly what I've been telling everyone since the beginning. This club isn't going to last unless we change the course we've been on. You were talking about the fear of losing what this club had built; let me tell you, we haven't built shit. We're damned near broke and have been for eight years. Cutter had to call in every outstanding debt to the club just to raise the capital needed for this phase of the plan. Nicky, this is it. We've got to figure out new, clean ways to earn or there will be no Burning Saints at all. Either this family learns to change, or we scatter to the wind."

For the first time I really began to understand the weight of Minus' newly fitted crown. He was right, and I'd probably always known it, but didn't want to admit it. Ours was a dying breed and you could see evidence of that everywhere. Lack of evidence more like it. We saw fewer and fewer riders on the road with each passing year, and with the gentrification of Portland now in full swing, outlaws and freaks were being pushed out at break-neck speeds. I see "Keep Portland Weird" bumper stickers on mini vans driven by the very soccer moms who complain about the noise from the local bars they chose to move next to. Cutter saw the writing on the wall, while the rest of us were busy fucking and fighting. Like a good President and leader, he was looking to the future, and he chose Minus as the Aaron to his Moses.

"Well, shit!" I snapped to attention. "Our Catholic school education got into me more than I'd realized," I said.

"What?" Minus asked, looking puzzled.

"I'm sorry for being a dick. I was glad to have you back from exile, and I guess I figured things would kind of go back to the way they were. Boy, was I fucking wrong." We both laughed. "With all the Los Psychos shit that went down, and then Cutter dying…I don't… I'm not good with words like you, and I feel like a fucking idiot talking about this shit."

"Nicky, you don't have to say anything. You've had my back through all of it, regardless of your own feelings. That's loyalty. That's what makes you who you are, and that's who I want as *my* Sergeant."

"Shit, man, you really did get all Zen down there in Savannah, didn't you?"

"You have no idea. C'mon, let's get inside and fill

these knuckleheads in on the plan," Minus said.

"We have a plan?"

"As far as they know, we do," Minus said smiling as he opened the door. "By the way what's your plan?"

"If you didn't come up with one, how the hell should I have?" I asked.

"No, not about Kitty. What's your business plan, for the club?"

"You wanna talk about that now?" I asked, scanning the room for the other Saints.

"You were the one that was pissed I didn't ask at Church."

"There's Big Pecker, over by the pool tables," I said, steering our conversation to the present. Although, it would likely only take ten seconds for Minus to shoot down my business proposal, we didn't have the time for me to call him an asshole and throw shit around.

"I see him," Minus said and we walked toward our compatriots.

"How could you fuckin' miss him?" I said, and Minus laughed. Big Pecker, and Little Pecker were two of our newest recruits, temporarily named according to their size and current standings within the club. If they should prove themselves useful, loyal, and worthy they could both one day wear a Burning Saints member's patch and be given a proper club name. Until then, they held a value to me that ranked just above a roll of paper towels.

Clutch

SALLY ANNE'S PLACE was dead at this time of day, so apart from a few late lunch stragglers, we pretty much had the place to ourselves to talk and plan before we headed out.

As we approached our group, I could see Wolf seated in the corner with one leg propped up on Little Pecker's thigh while he knelt before him. Little Pecker was shining Wolf's boot, and it looked like it took every ounce of his strength to get the job done. His scrawny arms waving like Kermit the Frog as he furiously buffed.

"What the fuck is this?" Minus asked.

Big Pecker was standing table side, holding a bridge

cue and what looked like a scotch on the rocks, while Ropes shot a game of pool by himself.

"The Peckers here were just showing they understand the meaning of the word service," Wolf said, taking a sip from his beer.

"Well, how 'bout you show me the meaning of the words, get to the fuckin' table and let's get to work," Minus growled.

We sat at our reserved corner table, which was in an alcove, set apart from the rest of the dining area. When the Saints bought the place, we redesigned some of the building to fit our needs as a club. We then sold twenty five percent of the place to Sally Anne, who runs it as an equal partner. Her blood, sweat, and tears more than make up for the other twenty five percent, and she can rest easy knowing that no one from the neighborhood is ever gonna fuck with her or her place.

"Okay, here's the deal. We're gonna hit Kitty fast and hard. We know where he lives and have a spotter on sight to verify that he'll still be there when we arrive. Clutch will be packing and the rest of us will have tasers," Minus said.

"And?" Wolf asked.

"And, what?" Minus asked.

"Aren't you forgetting something?"

"Please?" Minus added.

"No, like information of what we might be walking into," Wolf grunted.

"No idea," Minus said.

"And, we're squaring off against a possibly hostile, homicidal giant, simply because those pussy Fire Dogs told you to?" Wolf asked dryly.

"Yes, Wolf, the Dogs of Fire have asked for a return favor. I'm not sure what Kitty's got up his sleeve, or how he may be prepared for us. I just know that we've been charged with grabbing him and getting a computer key code from him. This information is gonna help the Dogs get their boy Hatch outta jail. Apart from Kitty's location, that's all the information I've got. The only thing you need to know is that there's a Wolf that needs to fetch a fucking Kitty, so let's go."

Wolf glared at Minus and got up slowly. As we left, the new redheaded waitress, the one that Minus had assumed I was banging, walked by, toward the bar with a tray of clean bar glasses. Minus turned and looked at me puzzled. He opened his mouth to speak, but I cut him off asking "We taking Five or surface streets?"

Minus shot me a look while calling out to the others. "You guys go on out to the bikes, we'll be there in a second," he said before turning back to me. "I thought she was back at your place."

"For the record, I never said anything. You were the one that made assumptions." I said.

"Then who was that at your place this morning?" he asked.

"Who said there *was* anyone?" I replied.

"I did, due to the fact that you were being cagey with me, and that you were MIA for most of the picnic," Minus said.

My eyes shot to his.

"Yeah, I noticed," he said. "It's kinda what got my curiosity up. What else, other than a new woman on the hunting grounds, could pull you away from a club picnic?"

"Ants. I fucking hate ants," I replied dryly.

"I guess I assumed that with "Red" showing up at the picnic on Friday night, and her being just your type and all, it was her. But now that I think about it, there was another new face at the picnic on Friday. Someone we all know and love, but who's never been to the compound before."

"Look, Minus—"

"But that couldn't possibly be who you snuck off with,

because you were specifically told to stay away from her."

"That's right," I said. "So, it couldn't be her."

Minus stared me down, before ending the conversation with, "Then I suppose the mystery continues."

We rode out to Kitty's location and checked in with Sweet Pea, who Minus had sent out earlier as a scout.

"He's still in there," he said.

"You sure, Pea? I don't want to go in there to find him gone and a booby trap left in his place."

"His place could be booby trapped?" Big Pecker asked, a little too loudly.

"Shut the fuck up, Man Tits," Wolf growled.

"Lay off him, or you and I are gonna have a problem Wolf," I snapped.

"You a titties man, Clutch?" Wolf said, smirking.

"Lay off, or the next time you have a titty in your mouth, it'll be through a straw," I replied.

"Both of you, save it for Kitty. You're gonna need all that piss and vinegar for him. Let's go. Follow me and keep it down."

Sweat Pea led us up to Kitty's apartment and I pulled out my 9mm. Wolf, Ropes, Sweet Pea, and Big Pecker all had their stunning devices set to go. Little Pecker was set to stand as lookout in the hallway. We also had cable ties, cuffs, and a vial of Thiopental I'd procured from a chick I knew that worked at the Portland Zoo. This shit could drop a rhino, so I knew it'd be just fine for Kitty if it didn't kill him.

"Okay, on three," Minus said. "Three, two—"

"That's a new door, and I'd rather not replace it," a voice crackled through a hidden speaker.

"Kitty?" Minus called out.

"Yeah, I can see you guys on my front door cam. I've also had eyes on the dipshit you posted out front for two hours. I figured you'd be by once I saw his patch. Let me buzz you in."

"Okay." Minus shrugged, and three dead bolts later, Kitty opened the door.

"Hey, Minus, come on in. What's up, Clutch? Wolf. Long time, guys," Kitty said smiling broadly as he shook each of our hands. His massive mitts covering ours.

"Not too much, Kitty. I was surprised to hear you were back in town," Minus said cautiously.

"So, you thought you'd throw me a surprise welcome back cattle prod party?" he asked, looking down at the electric pitchforks of the angry villagers.

"Hey, man, we just didn't know if this was a friendly neighborhood, you know what I mean?" Minus said.

"Or, you came here prepared to fuck my shit up, Burning Saints style," Kitty said.

"Sure, or that," I said.

"The question is, why?" Kitty asked, taking a seat. "Seriously, guys, you can put those down and relax. There's beer in the fridge, but please don't touch any of the gear."

I gave the guys the nod and collected their stun guns, which I placed back in my backpack. I looked around his shitbox apartment, and it was lined with racks of high end looking tech. The place looked like what NASA looked like…if it had taken up shop in a crack house.

"I know, the place is hell, but the rent is cheap, the neighbors keep to themselves, and until now, nobody knew where I was," Kitty said. "Which leads me to wonder how you found me, which then leads back to my first question, which still remains unanswered; why the fuck are you here, Minus?"

"I found you through the Dogs of Fire," Minus said.

"Oh, good," Kitty said enthusiastically.

"Good?" I choked out.

"Yeah, I have something for them."

"What's that?" Minus asked.

"I've been expecting Booker to reach out to me. I'll give it to him," Kitty replied. "I ascertain, you fine gentlemen are his official reach out."

"The Dogs said you have a key code that they need."

"Booker received and decoded my message. I'm glad to know he hasn't lost a step," Kitty said happily.

"So, let me get this straight. You wanted them to find you? And you're happy to give them the code they need?" Minus asked.

"Yep, that's right."

"Then why go through the trouble of helping Los Psychos frame Hatch in the first place?"

"Because, they paid me a shit ton of money, and because it got me back at the table in Portland. I also knew that I could leave a breadcrumb trail that Booker and the Dogs could follow but would leave Los Psychos in the dark."

"So, you're not running with Los Psychos?" I asked.

"Fuck those dirtbags. I've been using them to bankroll my new set up. I didn't need a tenth of this gear for the job they hired me for, but they don't know that. As a matter of fact, as soon as I'm clear of them, I'm going to activate a virus that I've imbedded at every level of their network. It's going to make every one of their laptops, servers, and cell phones become paperweights. I've also been running faulty backups for them without them knowing, so when all their data is fried, it'll be gone forever."

"What about a cloud backup?" Minus asked.

"Oh, you mean the account I set up that's really sending all their data to a nice group of Russian gentlemen I know? They have instructions to extort every penny they can from Los Psychos once I give the word, and once they pay, they'll delete the data anyway. Los Psychos won't be able to do a damn thing about it, and I'll be in the clear."

"That's some cold-blooded shit, Kitty," I said.

"I've learned to channel my rage to more positive

streams," he replied.

"I'm not sure that killer Mexican biker gangs and Russian hackers are positive streams, but point taken," I said.

"Believe me when I tell you that Los Psychos are merely cogs in the wheel of my plan."

"What plan is that?"

"To ride with the Dogs of Fire again," Kitty replied as serious as a fuckin' heart attack.

"That may prove to be a little problematic, Kitty. The Dogs are about as pissed at you as Los Psychos are gonna be."

"Trust me, I know how to handle Los Psychos, and from what I hear, you do, too. Be careful. They have a hard-on for the Dogs of Fire, and a super hard-on for the Burning Saints, so you both need to watch your backs."

"Yeah, we kind of figured that. Any ideas on what they have planned for us?" Minus asked.

"Plenty of ideas, but none of the kind that come for free," Kitty replied.

"We can pay you, what's the price?"

"You seem to be in tight with the Dogs of Fire, you get me back in with them and I'll tell you everything I know about their plans against your club."

"Jesus Christ himself isn't tight enough with the Dogs of Fire to get you back in with them," Minus replied.

"Then let me ride with you. I haven't ridden with a club since the Dogs kicked me out, and it'll give them a chance to see I've changed."

"I don't know, Kitty. Crow and Hatch would lose their shit on me if I let you ride with us. We're supposed to get the code and get you outta here."

"Well, Minus, the way I see it," Kitty said grinning from ear to ear. "You've got two choices. I can either give you the code key for free, and we can all ride out of here together, or you can try and redistribute those glow sticks before I start tearing into you and your boys."

* * *

Gina

This must be what a teenage boy feels like sneaking out of his girlfriend's room.

I quietly gathered up my stuff and slinked out Clutch's sliding door that led to his side yard. I could hear Clutch's muffled voice, and hoped he'd stall long enough for me to make my escape. The last thing I wanted was to get Clutch in trouble or to ruin my doctor/patient relationship with Minus and the club.

Oh, shit! Did I just sleep with a patient?

I racked my brains and was surprised to realize that I'd never treated Clutch for so much as a flu shot. He'd been around the clinic with Cutter, but never for himself. I suppose the fact that I didn't have a chart for him explained why I didn't know his real name.

Oh, good. I didn't sleep with a patient. Just an outlaw biker. That's muuuch better.

I waited until I'd walked two blocks away before calling an Uber to pick me up just to make sure I was well out of sight. My hasty retreat had caused me to begin to "sober up" from the weekend's events. Fortunately, I'd have the rest of the day to recover, and then mentally beat myself up for every stupid thing I'd said and done over the past forty-eight hours.

"You know what? Fuck that," I said, forgetting to use my inner dialogue.

"I'm sorry. Am I going the wrong way?" my startled Uber driver cried out.

"No, I'm so sorry. I was just talking to myself. Too loudly, apparently. You're doing great. Five stars all the way," I said, giving him a thumbs-up. I was losing it, but I barely cared. I didn't want to go home and beat myself up for sleeping with a biker. It felt good to be with Clutch. Really good, and I was a grown-ass, single adult, who had every right in the world to have a perfect stranger ram himself into my cock-starved pussy if I wanted.

I began to replay the events of the weekend in my mind and felt myself getting wet all over again. Never had the mere thought of a man, any man, made my body react like this. My attraction to Clutch was rooted in some sort of primal urge. As much as I was mentally starting to shut down and crave being back at home, physically I burned more with each mile that came between us. My phone buzzed, and I laughed when I saw an incoming text from N. Chriznowskovitz, esq.

N.: Just wanted to make sure U R OK.

Gina: I'm fine. In a car, headed back to my place. You're a lawyer now?

N.: No, I'm a criminal. That's how I was able 2 steal UR phone and change my contact name. The esq. comes in handy when U R sleeping with a Dr.

Gina: Thank you for this weekend.

N.: The weekend's not over. Dinner tonight?

Gina: Not a good idea.

N.: Eating dinner is a bad idea?

Gina: Not what I meant.

N.: Dessert?

I sat for a moment trying to think of a way out before realizing that I didn't want one. The only thing I wanted to do (well, not the *only* thing) was to have dessert with Clutch who, from what I could see, was a kind, thoughtful, caring person. When we were together, I saw little to no traces of the scary biker man I'd perceived him as. In fact, I was having a very hard time remembering him in that light at all.

Gina: Okay.

I hit send and swallowed hard.

N.: I'll text you later and swing by your place.

What the hell have I gotten myself into?

ELEVEN

BURNING SAINTS

Clutch

WE'D STOPPED FOR gas, so I'd taken a few moments to text the doc. I only meant to make sure she was okay, but before I could help myself, I'd asked her out to dinner. I didn't know what was wrong with me. Minus was already suspicious, and here I was adding fuel to the fire. Why the fuck should I care if she's okay? Usually, the idea of some chick sneaking out without a word after mind-blowing sex would be great, but clearly Eldie wasn't just some chick. I slipped my phone into my pocket just as Minus approached.

"So, whatta you gonna tell Hatch?" I asked.

"About Kitty riding with us? I'm not sure that it matters much. I'm pretty sure no matter what I say, he's gonna go ape shit," Minus said.

"No fucking kidding," I said, topping off the tank, and replacing the fuel nozzle back on the pump."

"Make sure you use your business card and get a receipt," Minus said.

Great, more Burning Saints, Incorporated bullshit.

"Fuck me with a…with a…what the fuck are those things called? You know, those old timey wooden things where you slide the little beads to help you count."

"An abacus," Minus replied.

"Yeah! Fuck me with an abacus, Minus," I said.

"I know, I know. Just get a receipt and keep track of your miles," he said walking away.

We headed back to the Sanctuary to wrap up the mayhem of the annual picnic. I'd hoped to be out of there by seven o' clock at the latest. I wasn't sure how I'd be able to get away any earlier without tipping off Minus, but I knew I had to see Eldie again as soon as possible.

* * *

We finally wrapped up everything at the Sanctuary around 9:15, and I texted Eldie that I was on my way to pick her up. I rode back to my place first, so I could get changed and park Charlene in the garage, as she was gonna spend the evening in.

Eldie buzzed me up when I arrived and just about knocked me out when she came to the door. She always looked amazing regardless of what she was wearing. Granted, I'd never once seen her in anything more formal than a doctor's coat, yet she always looked like a movie star. Tonight was no exception. She was dressed in jeans and a dark blue hoodie with her hair in a ponytail, and she couldn't have been hotter if she were in a red cocktail dress.

"Will this be warm enough for riding tonight, or should I get a coat?" she asked.

"Charlene's back at home tonight," I replied.

"Aww," she said in a pouty voice, her bottom lip sticking out in a way that made me want to bite it.

"C'mon, beautiful," I said, putting an arm around her, guiding us toward the elevator.

We made our way downstairs and out to the guest lot where my 1971 Plymouth Barracuda was parked.

"Eldie, I would like to introduce you to Lucille," I said, motioning to my midnight blue beauty. "She's my pride and joy."

"Oh, great. I have yet another lady to compete with?" she asked.

"Trust me, Doc, you have no competition."

"I thought Charlene was your one true love," Eldie teased.

"She is, as far as bikes are concerned, but Lucille is my number one ride. The machine I've spent the most time and attention on, not to mention money. You wouldn't know it by looking at her fine ass now, but when I found her, she was in the roughest shape imaginable."

"Then, why did you buy her?"

"Because I could see the beauty hiding underneath all the rust and dents."

"How?" she asked.

I grinned. "That's my gift. I can look at a machine and know instantly if it's worth scrapping or fixing."

"And she was a fixer, huh?"

"Yes, she was. My Lucille," I said.

"'Anything built like that just gotta be named Lucille,'" Eldie said, quoting Cool Hand Luke.

"I'm sorry, how the hell do you know that movie?" I asked, utterly stunned.

"My dad was a huge film buff. After the divorce, we'd spend a lot of our weekends watching movies together," she said, with a sad smile.

"Your folks split up, huh? I'm sorry," I said.

"Thanks."

"You only saw your pops on the weekends? Was that some sort of custody thing?"

"No, I lived with him full time. He worked long hours during the week, so the weekends were about the only time I really got to spend any time with him," she said.

"What about your mom? Where was she?" I asked.

"Mom was…well, Mom was off taking care of Mom," she said in a detached tone.

"I'm sorry, I didn't mean to pry," I said, seeing that I'd hit a sore spot.

"No, it's okay," she said, putting her hand on my arm. "My dad began showing signs of early onset Alzheimer's when I was a freshman in high school. By my junior year, my parents' marriage was a wreck and my mom took off."

"Took off?" I asked, my face beginning to heat up.

"She said my dad's illness was more than she'd signed up for, and that she wasn't equipped to be a single parent, so she moved to an ashram in New Mexico, and served him divorce papers via the mail, a year later."

"What about you?" I asked, barely able to process what I was hearing. "How could she leave you?"

"Honestly, I don't think it was hard for her at all. She'd call on my birthday, and we'd see each other three or four times a year, but I don't think she ever really wanted to be a mother."

"Is that why you never had kids?" I asked, immediately regretting it. "I'm sorry, that's none of my fuckin' business whatsoever."

"It's okay," she said. "I don't usually talk about myself a whole lot. I kind of suck at it. I didn't mean to dump a whole ton of family history drama on you before we'd even gotten in the car."

"Speaking of," I said, happy for the subject change, "Shall we go?" I asked, opening the passenger door.

"Thank you," she said and slid in.

After getting Eldie in her seat, I spotted someone

standing near a small group of trees, at the other end of the guest parking lot. They were dressed in dark clothes, facing our direction, and remained totally motionless.

"Stay in the car," I ordered, and closed her door. I then began walking quickly toward the shadowy figure. Once I was about twenty-five feet away, I called out, "Can I help you with something, pal?" To which the person immediately turned in the opposite direction and ran away at full-speed. I couldn't see much in the darkness, but it looked like a man, well under six feet in height. The one distinguishing feature I was able to make out was a white dragon printed on the back of his jacket.

I walked back to Eldie, who was still waiting inside Lucille. I got in, fired her up, and took off in hope of spotting whoever this creep was.

"What's going on?" Eldie asked as I zoomed through the parking lot.

"I just wanted to show you how great Lucille handles in tight spaces," I said, as I headed toward the rear of her building, Lucille's tires screeching.

"I think I get the point!" Eldie screamed as she fumbled for her safety belt.

I made a hard left and spotted the dragon-clad creep moving between two of the complex's buildings. I slammed on the brakes and put the car in park.

"Stay here," I said firmly, got out and took off at top speed toward the creep, who spotted me and bolted; and when I say bolted, I mean Usain Bolt-ed. I gave up the chase after ten seconds when I could clearly see there was no way in hell I'd ever catch this fucker. I could move at a fairly good clip for a guy my size, but this prick was outworking me. He was wiry and small framed. And from the way he moved, I'd guess he was an athlete at some point in his life.

I took a few moments to catch my breath and turned to head back to the car only to find that someone had snuck up on me. I pulled from my waistband and leveled my 9mm at whoever was trying to get the drop on me.

* * *

Gina

Cheesecake.

When Clutch asked me out for dessert, I thought the most dangerous thing I would face tonight would be the number of calories in a slice of cheesecake. If I was being honest, the order on tonight's potential threat list was Clutch's enormous dick then cheesecake, but those were certainly the only things that had come to mind. Boy was I wrong.

Everything started out nice enough. Clutch put me in the car... he'd even opened the door for me, which I thought was sweet. Then the next thing I knew he was shoving me in, running around or driving around the parking lot like a maniac. He'd currently left me stranded, car still running, with his door swung wide open, in the middle of an access road after taking off on foot between two buildings. I was terrified. I had no idea what the hell was going on. Did this have something to do with the Burning Saints? Was I in danger? Was Clutch Batman?

I sat frozen for a moment before I realized that it was mild-mannered Gina who was scared. *Eldie* was a bad-ass biker bitch, who didn't take any guff, and clearly needed to work on her tough-chick biker talk. Either way, I was getting out of this car and finding out what the fuck was going on.

I jogged in the direction I saw Clutch go, and it wasn't long before I could see what looked like his silhouette, barely lit in the alleyway. I began walking slowly and silently, as I still had no idea what I was walking toward. In fact, I was now wondering why I was out here in the first place. I could now barely see the Burning Saints logo on the back of Clutch's kutte and was about to whisper his name when he suddenly turned, pulled a gun, and pointed it directly at me.

"Holy shit, Doc," I heard Clutch say, through what sounded like a long tunnel, and my vision began to blur and darken.

The next thing I knew I was in Clutch's muscular arms, feeling like I'd just had the most glorious nap ever. Every muscle in my body felt loose and relaxed.

"Doc are you okay?"

"I'm great," I said, smiling, my eyes adjusting to my surroundings. It was then that I remembered where I was, and exactly what'd just happened.

"You pulled a gun on me!" I squealed, scrambling to my feet. "You…you pulled a gun on me…and…and…I passed out."

"You might want to keep it down a little," Clutch said, shushing me. "Your neighbors and all."

"Keep it down?" I whisper shouted. "You pointed a loaded gun at my head. Well, I assume it's loaded." I could barely make out Clutch's nod in the darkness.

"Perhaps a little less *alktay* about the *ungay* out here in *ublicpay*," he whispered back.

"Uckfay uyay Utchclay!" I said, as I rose to my unsteady feet and turned back for the car. At least, I hoped I was headed in the right direction. With having just fainted, the lack of light, and the fact that I'd been wearing an old pair of glasses since breaking my good ones during the accident, I could very well have walked right into a wall.

"Doc, please wait. It's not safe," Clutch said, coming up from behind.

"Stay away from me," I snapped as I picked up my pace down the alley. "And don't follow me."

"Eldie, please, he's still out here. Just stay close to me please," he pleaded as he kept up with my pace.

I turned to find myself face to chest with Clutch. He'd worked up a light sweat and smelled amazing. I was finding it harder and harder to resist full-on animal urges when I was around him. Even now, when terrified, I was still drawn to him in every way. This revelation was terrifying.

"Who were you chasing?" I demanded

"I don't know who he is, that's why I'm out here and why you need to stay in the car while I look for him."

"If you don't know who he is, then why are you running after him with a gun?"

"Let's just get back to Lucille and we can talk more about this," he said, pressing me forward, giving me no chance but to go with his flow.

"I'm not getting back in that car, or any car, with you," I said as we reached the end of the alley.

It seems I wouldn't have to worry about that, as the spot in the road where Lucille had been previously, was currently vacant.

TWELVE

BURNING SAINTS

Clutch

ELDIE, DID YOU park Lucille someplace?" I turned to face her, and she looked as surprised as me, but said nothing, which made my blood run cold. "Eldie, did you move the fucking car?" I shouted.

"No," she replied, "I left Lucille, running right here where you left her."

"I left her with you. You left her here alone, and now she's fucking gone!" I bellowed.

"You left me alone, in a running car while you ran off to chase whoever the hell it was you were chasing!" she yelled back.

"Look, we have to get off the street and get you to a

safe place. I have no idea who this creep is or what he wants."

"Looks like he wanted your car," she snapped back sarcastically.

"I don't think this is about the car, but I swear to God, when I find who took her," I stopped myself before I scared Eldie anymore. She was already looking at me like a glass of spoiled milk. All the better, really. This little escape from reality, or whatever the fuck Doc and I were doing, had to end. She may as well get a little glimpse into my fucked-up life and see the monster that I truly am.

"Look, Clutch. Whatever you're doing here, I want nothing to do with it. You asked me out for dessert, not to play robbers and robbers in the middle of the night. I've had more than enough adventure for one weekend and I'm going to walk back to my building now," Eldie said, and started to march back down the access road toward her place.

What the fuck could I do? She was right to be pissed and scared, and the last thing I wanted to do was make things worse, but there was no way in hell I was going to let her walk back to her condo alone. I thought about it for a moment before saying, "Okay, Doc. I understand. Have a good night. I'll see you around."

"I hope not," she replied without looking back.

"I'll text you and make sure you got home safely," I called out.

"Delete my number from your phone," she yelled back as she disappeared around the bend.

As soon as she was out of sight, I cut back the way I'd just come, between the two complex buildings, heading toward Eldie's unit. I made sure I stayed out of sight but kept her in mine. If this guy was more than a car thief, there was no way I was going to let him near the Doc. I followed her all the way to her building until I saw her enter the secured front door, before turning and making my way toward the freeway, dialing Ropes for a lift on the way.

* * *

Gina

"That's what you get for pretending to be something you're not, Gina," I said out loud to an empty condo. How could this have gone any other way? I mean, really, what did I expect? I was simply not cut out for wild nights and bad boys. Apparently, I also sucked at being a wife that was married to a stable, normal guy. A few days ago, the thought of being divorced from David made me feel like a free woman, and now I just felt like a failure in an empty condo.

I pulled out my phone and pulled up Clutch's contact. I smiled, but was struck with sadness when I saw his contact name "N. Chriznowskovitz, esq." How in the world did he go from knight in shining armor to guy in dark alley pointing gun so quickly? My thumb hovered over the 'Delete Contact' button for what felt like an eternity before I huffed in frustration and shoved my phone back in my pocket.

I grabbed a bottle of wine, and an opener from the kitchen and headed for my bedroom. I didn't bother bringing a glass.

* * *

Clutch

It had been a week since I'd had any contact with Eldie, and two weeks since we'd dropped her Jeep off at the Clinic. She'd asked that I not be the one to deliver it, and although it felt like the biggest dick punch ever, I agreed and had Mayday's guys handle it.

Even though Eldie and I had only spent a weekend together, I missed her. I missed her in a way that scared the shit out of me, and the more I thought about how badly I'd screwed things up, the shittier it made me feel. I couldn't believe that I'd laid into her about Lucille. That I'd actually tried to lay the blame on her for my dumb ass. This was the reason I didn't have a family, and never would. I didn't deserve one. I was a bad guy, and bad guys don't get to ride off into the sunset with the good girl, despite whatever fantasy land Minus was living in with Cricket.

Cricket.

A thought occurred to me that she might be able to help. Not with the Eldie situation. I knew I'd shot any chance of that to hell, not to mention she was still on Minus's 'no fly' list, but she might be able to help me with Minus himself.

Minus had texted me and the other officers, earlier. He said he was ready to discuss our business plans now that all seemed quiet on the Los Psychos front, and the chaos of the picnic was over. I was confident that Minus was going to hate my idea, but perhaps Cricket could give me some insight into how to best get through to him. As close as Minus and I once were, I knew that she knew and understood his current state of mind better than anyone.

I pulled out my phone and hit Cricket's contact icon. She answered right away.

"Hey, Clutch. Is everything okay?" She asked.

"Yeah, sure. Why wouldn't it be?" I asked, surprised by her question.

"Oh, no reason, it's just that you've never called me before, so I was a little surprised to hear from you, that's all."

I thought about it and she was right. I never had called her. Every club member and associate were programmed into our phones but, although I liked Cricket, I'd always tried to steer clear of her unless absolutely necessary.

"Yeah, well, I was wondering if you and I could have lunch or something?" I asked, nervously.

"Lunch? You and me?" she asked.

"I sorta want to pick your brain about something. Are you free today?"

"Sure, yeah, that would be great," she said in her usual cheery tone.

"Sally Anne's at noon?" I asked.

"See you there, Clutch," she replied and hung up.

* * *

I arrived at Sally Anne's a little early, to find Cricket already sitting at the club's private table.

"Of course, you're already here," I said as I approached.

"My brother always told me, "Early is on time, on time is late, and late is unacceptable," she said, in a deep, mock "Hatch voice."

"Speaking of your brother," I said. "Has Minus told him about Kitty yet?"

"He and Hatch *discussed* that very topic last night, as a matter of fact," she replied.

"And how did that go," I asked.

"Minus is at home nursing a black eye and bruised ribs, and last I heard the doctor was checking Hatch's foot for a possible fracture."

"A fractured foot?" I asked. "What the fuck were they doing, Kung-Fu fighting?"

"I have no idea, I just know that they're both idiots and are going to have to learn how to get along better," she said.

To which I added, "In order for the club's partnership to continue."

"No, in order for me not to kill both of them," she countered. "They're both acting like children and I'm about to break both of my feet off... in their asses, if they don't knock this shit off."

I was starting to like Cricket a lot more.

"So, what did you need my advice about? Is this about Eldie?"

What the fuck?

The new cute red-headed waitress, whose name I could now see was Devlin by her nametag, came to take our orders. We let her know what we'd like to eat and drink through polite smiles, mixed with a little chit-chat, but as soon as she'd finished up with us and was out of range, I shot right back to Cricket.

"What are you talking about?" I asked.

"I assumed that you wanted to talk about what to do about Eldie," she replied, casually laying her napkin on her lap.

Maybe I wasn't gonna like her so much after all.

"I came here to ask for your advice about Minus. Why would you think I wanted to talk about the Doc?"

"Aside from the fact that you couldn't take your eyes off her at the picnic?" she replied "Then again, how could anyone miss her after you'd become her personal shopper. Seriously Clutch, you gave her an extra-small T-shirt to wear. I expected better of you."

I felt a sting of guilt, but also a sense that Cricket genuinely cared about me. The fact that she'd set any kind of expectation for my behavior somehow made me feel good.

"I know, I was just goofing around at first, but you're right. I shouldn't have done that. I apologize," I said.

"You can apologize to her the next time you're out with her," she said.

"Who said anything about going out with her? I gave her a ride and a shirt after her fender bender and that's that," I said.

"So, the fact that she left and then you disappeared right afterwards was just a coincidence?"

I shifted in my seat while trying to find a convincing excuse knowing full well that this chick had me pegged.

Cricket looked me in the eyes and said, "Clutch, I know we don't know each other very well, but I'll make you a pledge right here and now, and I swear that I will never be the one to break it. I promise that you can tell me anything, and that I will never repeat a single word of it to anyone, unless I have your express permission to do so. Not even to Minus."

I stared intently at Cricket, trying to do my best to determine exactly what she was all about.

She continued, "I do not ask that you do the same, only that you never lie to me. If you do, I'll know it, and our bond of trust will be broken. Can we make that deal? Can you be straight with me?"

I nodded silently, and Cricket called out to Devlin, "Sweetie, bring us two shots of Jameson when you come back, will ya?"

* * *

Gina

I was *starving*. I usually hated it when people used that term, but I honestly felt like I could and would eat any food-shaped item placed in front of me. A decorative bowl of wax fruit wouldn't currently stand a chance.

"Maggie, the schedule's clear for the next forty-five minutes so I'm gonna run out and grab lunch. Do you want anything from the Taco Factory?" I asked my nurse as I grabbed my purse.

"It's the middle of the day," she said with an air of disgust in her voice.

"That's when people usually have lunch," I replied with a laugh.

"Yeah, but not at the Taco Factory. That place is strictly for 'after clubbing hours.' I'd accept it as a hangover meal as well, but it's certainly reserved for post-drinking only.

"Well, three crispy carnitas tacos with extra cilantro sounds perfect to me right now," I replied, heading out the door.

"Don't even bring that devil's lettuce back here with you!" she yelled as the door closed behind me.

I unlocked my newly repaired Jeep and as I opened the door, heard a familiar rumble in the distance. As the sound got closer there was no mistaking it was Charlene, and I looked up to see Clutch ride by. My heart didn't so much skip a beat as it stopped entirely, and I felt a sudden sense of loss and longing. I imagined Clutch making a sharp left turn and pulling into the clinic parking lot. I could clearly picture him taking off his helmet and smiling at me before saying something sexy like, "Hey there Doc, you wanna go get some *tacos?*" Jebus, I needed tacos and to stop thinking about the charming, sexy, gun waiving criminal that somehow had a direct line to my juice box.

Clutch didn't pull into the parking lot. In fact, he didn't even turn his head in my direction. He simply rode on, and that's what I needed to do, for the last time. In that moment, I resolved myself to putting Nikolai 'Clutch' Christakos out of my mind permanently.

I got in my Jeep, started it up and turned on the satellite radio. "Don't Need Ya" by Melody Morgan was playing and I turned up the volume. Perfect timing for a post-breakup anthem. Not that Clutch, and I had broken up, because we were never together in the first place, but…

Stop thinking about him!

I cranked the volume to the max and pumped up the bass; pushing the Jeep's speakers to the limit, as I sang along, "This is my life, and I'm sayin' bye bye, I'm sick of your lies, so look right in my eyes. I don't need ya, I don't want ya, I never needed you anywaaaaaaay," I belted out before putting the Jeep in reverse and backing out only to see Clutch in my rearview mirror, standing directly behind my Jeep.

"Oh my God!" I screamed as I slammed on my brakes.

"Sorry," he called out. "I didn't mean to scare you."

I opened the door and flew out of the car. "I could've

run you over. What were you doing sneaking up on me like that?"

"You were in there singing away, I didn't expect you to back out so suddenly. You really are dangerous when you're doing carpool karaoke, aren't you?" he asked with a smile.

That smile. *The* smile. The *please, please, please for the love of all things bend me over a chair and have your way with me* smile. I must be strong and resist.

"What do you want, Clutch, and why are you lurking around my clinic?"

"I wasn't lurking or sneaking, I swear. In fact, I just rode by and decided to stop in," he said.

"Where's your bike?" I asked.

"I…ah…I parked Charlene in the parking lot of the law firm next to you and walked over here. I thought maybe if you heard her pipes, or saw me coming, you'd go into your office and hide from me or something. And, Lucille's still missing, so I couldn't drive her."

I dropped my guard just a little. "Clutch, I'm really sorry about Lucille—"

"Doc, please don't say another word. I'm the only one that needs to apologize here. I was a total jackass and I should have never blamed you for Lucille. Leaving her in the street was my fault and it was stupid but leaving you like that is the biggest regret of my entire life." Clutch moved closer to me, but I wasn't afraid. The look in his eyes and the sound of his voice told me that I could believe him, but there was still no way in hell I could trust him.

"I appreciate that Clutch, I really do but—"

"Nicky," he said taking my hands. "Please call me Nicky. I don't want to be Clutch to you. I want you to forget you ever even met that guy."

"But you are that guy. Your life is dangerous and crazy. You pulled a gun on me, for crying out loud," I said.

"My other regret," he said, breaking contact. "I was trying to protect you. Without getting into too much detail, my club has enemies, and I'm pretty sure someone from a rival club was at your condo complex that night."

"This is supposed to make me feel better?" I asked.

"No, I'm just trying to explain myself a little, and to be more open with you," he said.

"Why? There's no 'us' to work on, and we both know that any attempt would be a bad idea. Besides, even if I wanted to be with you, and I don't, *you* can't because of Minus."

"Screw Minus and his rules, I can be with whoever I fuckin' want to be with." he said, puffing out his chest slightly.

"But I don't want to be with you, Clutch. Now, if you'll excuse me, I have a date with the best rice and beans in town."

"Doc, please, have dinner with me tomorrow night, and if you never want to talk with me again after that, I'll understand, and I swear you'll never see my face again."

He stood straight with the earnestness of a cub scout. I swear I'd never seen anything more adorable in my entire life.

"Dinner only," I said firmly.

"Eight o'clock okay?" he asked, to which I nodded. "I have a quick meeting beforehand, so I'll text you the address and meet you there if that's okay."

"Don't be late," I warned, and he simply smiled back.

His charm was infuriating.

* * *

Clutch

I felt like I was trying to woo two women. Later, I'd be focusing on Eldie, but right now I had to close the deal with Minus. More accurately I had to pitch the deal and not have him laugh me out of the room. He'd been meeting with each of the officers one-on-one regarding our business ideas, which was fine by me. The fewer fucking meetings in my life the better. Besides, I didn't need a whole room full of assholes laughing at my dumbass idea.

"Hey, Nicky. Come on in," Minus said, looking up from his laptop.

"I still can't get over seeing you sitting at Cutter's desk, in his old office."

"You and me both. Cricket says we can order new furniture when the club starts turning a profit," he said.

"When's that supposed to be?"

"2037," he replied and we both laughed.

"Sit down, man. You want a beer?" Minus asked.

"Nah. I'm cutting down actually," I replied. "I'm hoping to have reason to stay closer to my fighting weight."

"You got a fight coming up?"

"No, but that's sort of what I want to talk to you about. About my business plan that is. I don't have a… fancy presentation or anything…I—"

"Nicky. It's okay brother. What the fuck are you so nervous about? Just talk to me."

It was then that I realized why I'd been so nervous about talking to Minus all along. It wasn't just because I was afraid he was going to shoot the plan down and I'd have to start at square one. It was because I really cared about this idea. I was starting to get excited and was scared Minus was going to take this opportunity away from me, just like he was trying to keep me from Eldie.

"I slept with the Doc," I blurted out, before I'd fully comprehended what I'd done.

"What the fuck?" Minus laughed.

"I slept with Eldie. Well, she slept with me…we slept *together* is the point. We wanted to, and we did," I said.

"Okay then," he replied. "What else?"

"What else?"

"Yeah, what else do you have for me? I assume that

sleeping with Doctor Gardner isn't how you plan on making money for the club. Unless she's paying you a shit ton of money to knock boots. Are you a gigolo?" Minus laughed.

"I thought you'd be pissed after all your warning to stay away from her."

"Did you listen?" he asked.

"No, but—"

"There ya go," he said.

"What the fuck is that supposed to mean?"

"Nicky, I've been friends with you long enough to know that even if I'm the club's president, you're never gonna listen to a goddamned word I say. I know you will always have my back, and I know you'll march when you need to march, but I'm realistic. I'd rather you not fuck up our relationship with Eldie, but you're an adult and I knew you were gonna fuck her the minute I saw you roll up with her at the picnic. You think I don't know you by now?"

"Fair enough, but just so you know, we're going out tonight. I like her Minus, a lot. She's not really into me at the moment, but I'm hoping tonight will change things, and it would be better for me if you were on my side rather than throwing up a roadblock."

"What the fuck am I gonna do? After the shit Hatch and Cutter pulled back in the day to keep me and Cricket apart, I'd be a dick if I stood in your way if you have real feelings for her. Truthfully, I'm glad for you. Maybe if you're happy, you'll be less of an insufferable prick. Don't fuck it up. Now, whatta ya got for me?"

"Like I said, I didn't write anything down, but I have some rough figures in my head and…fuck it. I want to open a combat sports gym. I found a building that would be perfect, and by my rough estimates think we could be profitable in just under a year. You said there had to be a community service aspect, so I think we could do volunteer work training at-risk kids after school and shit." I said the words out loud for the first time ever and mentally braced for the sting of Minus' rejection.

"Sounds great. I love it," was all he said.

"That's it?"

"No, that's not it. Not even close. You'll need to get with Cricket, work out the actual numbers with her and make sure we can get approved for whatever loans we need, but I think the idea is solid and that you'd be great at running a gym."

"I thought you'd think I was just looking for an excuse to punch people in the mouth," I said, still stunned. "I even met with Cricket beforehand, I was so sure you'd hate the idea."

"Smart move. What did she tell you?"

"To be direct and honest."

"That's my woman," he smiled.

THIRTEEN

BURNING SAINTS

Gina

I STOOD OUTSIDE the Pink Priest, or more accurately paced, for forty-five minutes. A steady flow of patrons entered and exited, as I waited, like an idiot in an outfit I felt five years too old and ten pounds too heavy to be wearing. I checked my phone for any missed messages from Clutch and had decided to leave before I heard his voice call out, "Hey, Doc!"

Even though I was not pleased with his lack of punctuality, his smoky voice made my lady parts ache. I, however, wasn't about to let him know that, so I turned around sharply to face him and made sure to wear my mood plainly on my face.

"Sorry, I'm late. Please don't shoot," he said, putting

his hands up. "I was talking to Minus, and—"

"I'm freezing, my feet are killing me in these stupid shoes, and I'm starving," I barked out like a lunatic.

"Well, shit, baby, let's get you inside. You didn't have to wait out here."

"Don't baby me, and don't tell me where I can and cannot wait. When I'm invited out, I don't go into restaurants alone. I wait to be escorted, like a lady, by a gentleman," I said, barely able to believe the words coming out of my mouth were my own. Clutch said nothing, but blinked several times, before placing his hand on my shoulder and gently guiding me away from the curb to a more private spot behind a row of potted birch trees.

"Doc, what are you doing?" he asked.

"What do you mean? You're late and I'm pissed," I replied.

"Yeah, but I apologized for that, and that's not really what I'm talking about," he said.

"What do you mean?" I asked, suddenly feeling like I'd been thrown off balance.

"I mean, you're giving off a pissed-off girlfriend kind of vibe here," he said.

"Because I'm angry that you're late for our date, and that I've had to stand out here in the cold, not knowing if you'd even show up!"

"See, that there is what I mean. Calling this a *date*, saying you expect to be escorted by a *gentleman*. That kind of shit."

"Shit?"

"I'm not saying that proper dates, and romance, and boyfriend/girlfriend…*stuff*, isn't great, it's just not really what I've been accustomed to doing in the past, or what you and I started out doing." Clutch leaned in close, and his eyes focused on mine a little longer than made me feel comfortable. But then again, Clutch didn't make me feel comfortable at all. "You're gonna have to give me a second to figure out how to do some of this. Is that okay?"

It was at that very moment that I realized that he didn't make me feel any way I'd ever felt before. It was some sort of mixture of rebellion and freedom. The lack of feeling in control around him wasn't because I didn't feel safe, it was because I was scaring myself with how free I was allowing myself to be. At first, being with Clutch meant that I didn't have to be Gina or carry around her baggage. I could simply be Eldie, and Clutch could be my secret sin, but now there was something more that I craved from him, but I didn't know what it was.

"You're right, I'm sorry," I said.

"Way too many fuckin' people are agreeing with me lately."

"What's wrong?" I asked, confused.

"First, Minus then Cricket. Now you tell me I'm right after I'm a jerk by being late. I can't keep up with this upside-down world I'm living in."

"What I mean is, you're right that I probably only know how to fight like someone in a full-on relationship. I married the first guy that I'd ever dated seriously and hated the thought of trying to navigate my way through the current hookup culture. All of this is new to me. I was trying to save my marriage when all the dating apps came out, and now I've proven myself incapable of even having a one-night stand without making it weird."

"Hey," he said, lifting my chin. "*I* was the one that asked *you* out tonight. I wanted to formally apologize, and to thank you properly for cleaning my house, shopping, and for everything. I had a really great time with you before things got weird, and for what it's worth, you never felt like a hook up to me. What I'm saying is I guess I'd like tonight to be a…"

"A date?" I asked

"It's whatever you want it to be, baby. Just promise you'll spend the evening with me tonight, and I promise

I'll never be late again," he said, crossing his heart over his Sgt's patch.

"I expect my friends to keep their promises," I said, pulling him down closer to me.

"Is that what we are? Friends?" he whispered, our lips inches apart.

"You betcha, Nicky."

He kissed me deeply, his massive arms wrapped tightly around my body, which was no longer shivering.

"C'mon, let's get inside. I could use a drink. You ever been here?" he asked while holding the door open for me.

"I didn't even know it existed until tonight," I admitted.

Clutch laughed. "You're in for a real treat."

We entered the Pink Priest and my jaw just about hit the glitter covered floors. The foyer of the restaurant was a hodgepodge of gold leaf and hot pink. The place looked like gaudy and elegant had a fistfight after drinking one too many lava lamps.

"Welcome to the Pink Priest, my name is Friar Chuck, the Maître'd, do you have a reservation with us this evening?" An extremely large bearded man, wearing a purple paisley robe and a white feather boa asked us.

"No, but I'm friends with the owner," Clutch said, to my surprise. "Is Bob here tonight?"

"*Robert* is here this evening, but he's not receiving…guests," Friar Chuck said in a dismissive tone after noticeably sizing up Clutch.

Clutch took Friar Chuck's meaty hand in his, discreetly slipping him a folded bill in the process.

"Do me a favor will ya, Padre? Let *Robert* know that his old buddy Clutch is here; and that he and his lovely *date*," he said looking at me, "would love to sit in the confessional tonight if that would be possible."

Friar Chuck glanced at the bill in his hand and said, "Please allow me to see what I can do," before shuffling off quickly.

"He moves pretty quick for a big boy," Clutch said, before adding, "especially in those heels."

"I should ask him for tips," I said looking down at the overpriced torture devices currently strapped to my aching feet.

"No use being in pain," Clutch said, plainly. "Why don't you take 'em off."

"Because they match my outfit perfectly," I said. "That's why I bought them. I've never had the chance to wear them, and I never get dressed up and go out anymore, plus I wanted to look cute tonight."

"Doc," Clutch said with a slow smile that lit up his usually sullen face. "You'd have to be beaten with the ugly stick for a week to get you down to cute. You look absolutely beautiful, and in a lot of pain." He bent down and gently unbuckled the strap on my left shoe, removing it before focusing on the right. The familiar blush of embarrassment crept up the back of my neck.

"What am I supposed to do now?" I asked. "I'll feel like an idiot walking around barefoot."

"Here, I'll take off my boots and we'll pretend that we're at a Japanese restaurant," he said, reaching down.

"No, don't you dare," I laughed, pulling on his muscular arm. "Didn't you see what happened in Donnie Brasco?"

"What did you just say?" Clutch asked.

"Oh, nothing," I said. "I was just referencing Donnie Brasco, it's an old Jonny Depp movie that no one ever knows about."

"That's my favorite movie of all-time," Clutch said.

"Shut up, you're totally lying," I said. "That is such a first date line."

"I'm lying? Fugetaboutit," Clutch said, doing a surprisingly good Al Pacino impersonation. "You think my story is a fugazi? Ask anyone around here about me, and they'll tell you, I'm known."

"Holy shit!" I squeaked out way too loud, before covering my mouth, causing both of us to laugh. "You really *do* know it."

"I told you, it's my favorite movie," he said.

"Okay, *Lefty*, but I'm still embarrassed," I said, wiggling my exposed piggies.

"Look around, Doc," Clutch said, waiving my heels in the air. "This ain't exactly the kind of place one can be easily embarrassed in."

"What is this place? Some sort of drag show?" I asked with a giggle.

"Not exactly," he said, just at Friar Chuck returned.

"We are preparing the confessional for you as we speak. Robert would love to join you both a bit later if that is alright with sir and madame."

"That would be great," Clutch said, slipping Friar Chuck another bill, and pulling him close before whispering something in his ear. Friar Chuck nodded and said, "Please allow one of our hosts to seat you and enjoy your evening with us, you beautiful sinners."

As our host led us through the main dining room, the feast for the eyes continued. Colorful lights were strung up everywhere, and the walls were adorned with velvet paintings the likes of Marilyn Monroe, Andy Warhol, and John Waters. Papier mâché heads of famous religious leaders were mounted and hung like big game trophies. Everyone from Friar Tomás de Torquemada, the Inquisitor-General of the Spanish Inquisition, who's mouth had been fitted with a ball gag, to televangelist mega-star Joel O'Sheen, his typically fluorescent white smile, painted an irreverent hot pink. Whoever decorated this place had an obvious disdain for organized religion. Everywhere the eye landed, was some sort of visual dig on church, or its leadership.

We came to a heavy wooden door at the far end of the dining room that lead us to a much smaller room with rough stone floors. The space had no windows and couldn't have been more than ten feet by ten feet. The room was furnished with a small table and two chairs and was lit only by candlelight. Not romantic candlelight mind you, but more like a gothic castle, creepy Dracula shit. We were seated by two silent figures in robes adorned with pink sequins, who then left us alone.

"Okay, what the night-of-the-living-drag-queens is going on around here?" I asked.

"Shhh, don't call them drag queens," Clutch whispered. "I told you before, this isn't a drag show, and these guys can be a little touchy about labels."

"An ogre in a tiara named Friar Chuck cares about labels? Tell me, did the Franciscan brothers give him the name Chuck or was that his birth name?"

"Choosing a name, or identity for yourself, is not the same as having a label put on you, trust me," Clutch said.

"I thought you didn't get to choose your own names in your club?" I asked.

"True, but I choose to be a biker, to ride with the Burning Saints, and to abide by the club's rules, so ultimately answering to the name Clutch is my choice," he replied.

"Okay, but was being "labeled" Sergeant at Arms your choice, or was that thrust on you?"

"I'll tell you about *thrusting it on you*," Clutch said with a smirk.

"Don't change the subject," I said.

"The Sergeant's patch was "bestowed" upon me, as it were," he replied.

"How?" I pressed.

"During church, about three months after Rusty passed away—"

"Poor thing. Rusty was a sweet old guy."

"Rusty was a cold-hearted bastard that would break someone's leg for a dollar and give you back change. He also taught me a lot about living, and even more about dying. Anyway, Rusty was barely in the ground, and Cutter pointed the staff at me and said out loud to the room, 'Anyone here that's got a problem with young Clutch picking up Rusty's patch better come to me with a good fuckin' reason, right here and right fuckin' now.'"

"He didn't ask you beforehand?"

"Never mentioned a word. In fact, I'm not even sure he'd uttered more than ten words directly to me. Until about two years prior I reported to Rusty, and then to Wolf."

"So why did he spring it on you?"

"Because that's the way Cutter started doing things at the end, real impulsively. At least that's the way it seemed at the time..." Clutch's words drifted off.

"So... a label *was* thrust upon you without consent?" I said, bringing him back.

"Yeah, I guess so, but that's different than what I'm talking about with these guys here."

I smiled. "Of course it is, but I got you to tell me something about you and your super-secret club."

"Pretty sneaky, Doc." He grinned. "Okay, then. I've got a question for you about Cutter."

"A question for *me* about Cutter? What could I possibly know about him that you didn't."

"I want to know what his form of payment was to you," he said.

"Payment? What are you talking about."

"No, no, no. Don't play games with me, Doc. The old man's dead. Time to spill the beans. I heard you guys talking about it a couple times, but he'd never tell me how it was he'd repay you for taking care of the club all these years. I know you'd never take money, so what was it?"

"None of your business," I said.

"So, I was right all along. It *was* sexual favors. Thanks, Doc, I just won five-hundred bucks in the club pool," he said, smiling.

"No, you pervert. It's just that it was something sweet and personal that he'd do for me. Well, not directly for me, but for others," I said.

"Cutter doing something sweet? Now I know you're lying," Clutch said, leaning back in his chair. His massive muscular frame looked like it was stressing the limits of the antique wood.

"It was more than sweet, if you want to know the truth. He saved lives," I said, and Clutch stopped smiling.

"What? Really?"

"Kids actually," I replied. "I'd never accept club money, because I figured however it was made was not exactly blood free, so whenever I'd patch up a club member, Cutter would make a sizable, and anonymous, donation to the pediatric oncology department at OHSU."

Clutch looked stunned.

"You *really* never knew about this?" I asked, surprised.

"Never heard a word about it. It's probably why the club is broke," he mumbled.

"What?"

"Nothing. Wow, that's crazy. He helped a lot of kids then, huh?"

"All the Burning Saints did, when you think about it," I replied.

"I guess so," he said, looking a bit proud.

"So, how do you know the owner of this, whatever this place is?" I asked.

"The Saints have known 'Robert the Oral' since way back before there was a Pink Priest.

"Robert the Oral?" I asked with a giggle.

"Yeah, Bob's kind of anti-religion."

"I sort of noticed the theme," I said, smirking.

"Yeah, well he's especially down with people he sees as 'profiting off the word of God.'"

"So, is he some sort of true believer?" I asked.

"Ha, ha, ha. No, Bob's about as atheist as they come, but full of love. He's not even angry at people of faith, just those who use religion for profit. He likes to give his staff titles that poke fun at famous people of the cloth. Once you meet him, you'll understand a little more."

"What's this place all about, then?" I asked, motioning to our surroundings.

"Mostly, the Pink Priest is a restaurant, and a damned good one at that. Bob is a kick ass chef."

"Wow, he's the head chef as well as the owner?"

"After culinary school he worked in Paris and New York, but dreamed of opening his own, unique place in Portland, so we helped him."

"How did you become friends?" I asked.

"What do you mean?"

"Well, I assume he was a friend of the club's in order for you to want to help him get his restaurant off the ground," I replied.

"Doc, that's not quite the way my line of business works," he said, flashing his devilish smile.

"What do you mean?" I asked, leaning in closer, my curiosity now entering the red zone.

"Let's just say that without our club's help, this place couldn't have been built, let alone been able to thrive. I'll just leave it at that."

"You tease. You've got to tell me more than that," I protested.

"Not my story to tell," was all Clutch would say, and put his hands up.

"Okay then, let's go back to you becoming Sergeant at Arms," I said, before a tall, slender man, who I assumed was our server, came in.

"Clutch. Slam my heart into fifth gear. Jimmy heard you were here but we to see you with our own eyes to believe it," the man said as he burst through the door.

"We're not done with this," I whispered.

"Hey, Jimmy," Clutch said, getting up to embrace him. Clutch then brought Jimmy, who was dressed in a black and white checkerboard suit, over to the table. He wore a wire-framed top hat, that also doubled as a birdcage, complete with a tiny stuffed canary, perched inside.

"Jimmy Swagger, please meet Doctor Gina Gardner," Clutch said, about as formally as I'd ever heard him say anything.

Jimmy was a handsome African American man, with a clean-shaven head and deep-set eyes that sat behind bright red frames. He stared at me with an intense gaze, before simply, saying, "Doctor."

"Eldie is fine," I said extending my hand, which remained outstretched and untouched for what felt like an eternity as Jimmy's eyes remained locked onto mine. He said nothing, but I swear I felt him peering into my very soul. I began to feel my upper lip sweat and wondered if Jimmy could somehow read my thoughts. Just when I thought I'd crack from the intense awkward pressure, Jimmy clapped loudly and screamed.

"We love her!" he exclaimed, his surprise declaration making me jump in my seat. He smiled wide and leaned down for a huge hug.

"Robert is so happy you are here. He's preparing something amazing for the two of you for dinner. First, please allow us to make you both cocktails."

"Thank you, Jimmy," Clutch said, nodding.

"Yes, thank you," I replied. "I'll have a—"

"My dearest Eldie, Jimmy knows exactly what you want, more specifically, Jimmy knows exactly what you need," he said before turning on his Berluti's and exiting as swiftly as he entered.

"So, that was Jimmy," Clutch said, returning to his seat.

"And, Jimmy, among other things, talks about himself in the third person," I said, laughing.

"Yes, Jimmy does. He's also been Bob's husband for eighteen years, as loyal a person as they come, and is kind of a wizard with cocktails."

"I picked up on that as well. I'm also going to go out on a limb and guess he's also the one behind the décor."

"So, now that you know a little about the place and the people who make it tick, let me tell you why we're here," Clutch smiled and took my hand, a gesture of tenderness that I wasn't expecting. It's not like he hadn't been sweet to me thus far, but this simple act seemed somehow vulnerable. "Like I said earlier, I wanted to thank you for everything that you did back at my place, and to maybe explain myself a little." Clutch said softly.

"Explain yourself? What do you mean?" I asked.

"I don't know. Look, this is kind of weird for me. Explaining my feelings that is, and I thought maybe this place would make it easier somehow."

"How did you figure that? This place is like something out of a Fellini film," I laughed.

"True, the Priest has a certain chaotic energy to it, but the confessional was designed to be a place for two people to sit down and be honest with one another while sharing a meal."

"Sounds more like couple's therapy than a date," I said.

"Yeah, well, that's the thing…"

"Is this couple's therapy?" I squawked.

"No! Not exactly, but it's usually something that people that are much closer do together," Clutch said, letting go of my hand. "This was a bad idea," he said, getting up.

"No, it's fine," I said, reaching for his arm. "If this is the kind of thing that you usually do on a date then I'm willing to give it a shot," I said, trying my best to stow the utter terror I was feeling inside.

Intimacy was not something I was looking for here. I'd hooked up with Clutch because I thought it was just that, *a hook up.* I'll admit that I had some trouble getting off the bull once the ride was over, but I was a little afraid of where this was all going, and this bizarre atmosphere wasn't exactly helping.

Clutch sat back down. "No, that's just it. I've never taken anyone here and I haven't seen the inside of the confessional since the first time I was given a tour of the place."

"Then, why me?"

"That's the thing that's hard for me to say, exactly," he said, brushing a hand through his beard.

"Then say it, *inexactly,* please," I said. "Because I'm starting to feel a little weird about this whole thing."

"I guess I brought you here tonight because I feel comfortable with you," he said, looking satisfied with his answer.

"Wow, you do suck at this," I said, crossing my arms. "Please explain. Comfortable? Comfortable how? Like a new sofa or an old shoe?"

"Okay, take it easy," he said, to which I raised an eyebrow.

"Also, the wrong thing to say," he said, pushing away from the table, and rising to his feet once again. "Look, here's the deal. I like you Doc, and you make me feel… fuck…comfortable. Maybe that's a shitty word, but I'm not trying to insult you, I'm trying to compliment you. Comfortable is not a way that I've felt a lot in my life, far from it actually. I didn't have a family, and until the Saints, I never really fit in anywhere. Now, my club is changing, and I'm not even sure how I fit in there anymore. Until recently, I haven't been able to talk to my best friend about anything I've been going though because he was part of my problems. Usually I walk around feeling like there's a dark cloud hanging over my head, but when I'm around you I feel… different, and I guess I didn't want us to go any further before I told you that."

Gina

I FELT LIKE a bitch.

No, let me rephrase that. I felt like the biggest bitch ever. The utter shame and self-loathing I felt at that moment was like nothing I'd ever experienced. The courage that it must have taken Clutch to invite me here and open his heart like that, and my audacity to feel uncomfortable made me want to stab myself with one of the high heel shoes now in my purse. I was clearly some sort of emotionally detached robot person. My medical license should've been stripped from me on the spot.

I burst into tears.

"Jesus Christ, Doc! Are, you okay?" Clutch asked,

coming over to my side of the table, and placing his arms around me.

"Yes, I'm sorry, I don't know why I'm crying. What you said was so sweet, and unexpected, and...sweet."

"You said that already, Doc," he said, wiping the tears from my eyes, and gently kissing my forehead.

Jimmy returned with our drinks, flanked by two servers in matching hot pink leather uniforms who were each pushing carts. He immediately noticed that I'd been crying and shot a look at Clutch.

"What have you done? Why is the Queen crying, biker boy?" Jimmy asked in a voice I was sure would get him punched out cold.

"It's okay, Jimmy, it was actually self-induced, well sort-of. Clutch *did* make me cry...but only because he said some extremely sweet things to me," I said, blotting my tears with my napkin.

"If this *barbarian* doesn't treat you right, you just let Jimmy know."

Clutch, to my surprise, merely held his hands together and bowed to Jimmy.

"Thank you, Jimmy, he's been a perfect gentleman," she reiterated.

"Well, we hope he's not *all* gentleman," he said with a mischievous laugh. "Now, where were we? Oh, yes, cocktails!"

Jimmy went over to one of the carts and produced two beautiful concoctions. One, a beautiful blend of pink and orange hues, with a sugared rim, and the other bright green, served in a tall glass. To my surprise he set the pretty one in front of Clutch, and the other in front of me.

"The fuck is this thing?" Clutch asked.

"That, my dear boy is art. It's called a Trixie Sunrise," Jimmy said.

"It would've killed you to bring me a beer?" Clutch protested, running his hand down his face.

"It's not merely the presentation and taste of a cocktail that make it beautiful. There are also the drink's ingredients and their desired effects to take into consideration. Knowing the cocktail that someone will enjoy, whether they'll admit it, is one thing. Knowing the specific concoction, one needs without delay? That, biker boy, is the magic of Jimmy."

"Fair enough," Clutch said and took a sip. "It's sweet as shi...sh...sugar," he said.

"You need more sweetness in your life, Clutch," Jimmy said, smiling at me. "That's why we like her around. But don't worry, the tequila and other secret ingredients will take care of your inner savage beast."

"And mine?" I asked.

"That one, my dear, is called 'Kermit's Bad Day.'"

I dragged my straw through the thick green sludge and said, "I think I can see why. What's in it?"

"That, Jimmy's going to keep a secret for now, but we will say, be careful. It may not taste like it, but those things pack a punch."

I took a sip and decided that this was among one of the most horrific things I'd ever had in my mouth and that includes Matt Gilbert's tongue in the eighth grade. The overwhelming flavor of lawn clippings masked any and all traces of alcohol, which was a real shame.

"Well?" Jimmy asked, his eyebrows perched high above the top rim of his glasses.

"It's very...chunky," I said, forcing a smile.

"Remember, my Queen, Jimmy always knows what you need, so you drink all of that, you hear?"

I smiled and nodded, and Jimmy floated to the serving cart on the opposite side of the table which held what I assumed was tonight's dinner. Jimmy looked at me, then my glass, then back to me.

I took the hint, and another full swig of the slimy, green goop. I strained every taste bud to its very limit trying to detect a hint of any alcoholic spirit in hopes that it might somehow quell the putrid taste of swamp water. Kermit didn't just have a bad day. He'd contracted the swine flu and shit himself to death on his fucking lily pad.

"Good girl," Jimmy said as a small wave of nausea hit me and images of the aftermath of Earl's seven fish sandwich dinner flashed through my mind. Jimmy then lifted the dome on the tray to reveal an entire fish, head, tail, cloudy eyeballs, and all.

The confessional was in serious jeopardy of being violently redecorated in Kermit green.

"Excuse me," I said and ran for the door, which Jimmy raced to swing open for me as I made my frenzied exodus.

"The right! Keep to the right!" I heard Jimmy yell as I ran for the little nun's room, which thankfully was not far. I burst through the door, grateful to be the room's only current occupant. More importantly, it was good for any potential fellow restroom dweller that they were not present, as what happened next was not pretty.

After the demon had been sufficiently expelled from my stomach (perhaps this was a holy place after all), I picked myself up off the black and white tiled floors to go clean up.

On the opposite side of the room was a row of hot-pink pedestal sinks with an oversized gold-framed mirror hanging over each of them. The space looked like the Moulin rouge meets Wonderland. I gasped in horror at my reflection. My hair was stuck to my sweaty forehead and my eyes were blood-shot from throwing up so violently. Worse than that, my so-called water-proof mascara had run down my cheeks in dark wavy streams. The final insult was that I'd left my purse on the back of my chair when I'd run out of the confessional. Now I had no way to freshen up and was going to have to return to the table looking like I'd just sixty-nined a racoon in the ladies' room.

Great job, dumbass.

I don't know what happened. Normally it took a lot to get me to throw up, but I suppose the combination of Jimmy's green sludge, the fish head special, and the triggered memory of Earl losing his lunch on me, was all just a bit much.

Just as I began contemplating escaping through the window, I heard a knock on the bathroom door and Jimmy's voice call out, "Is the Queen alive?"

I laughed and replied, "Barely, come on in."

Jimmy came through the door holding my purse. "I thought you might need this," he said warmly, with no hint of dramatic affectation. I also caught his use of the word 'I' as it was the first time I'd heard Jimmy refer to himself in the first person.

"Thanks," I said. "Your drink was beautiful. I think it may not have agreed with me."

"My apologies, my queen. I should have warned you of possible...side effects. Kermit hit you much harder than I'd anticipated."

"I'm so embarrassed. I don't know what happened. I've been a little *off* lately."

"Let's get you cleaned up, shall we?"

"Thanks," I said. "I think I may need more tools than I have in this bag to repair the damage."

"Listen up, Dr. Hot Mess," Jimmy said, a twinge of the reverend Swagger, coming back to his voice. "You'd be gorgeous in a burlap sack, and I don't just mean wearing one. If you were stuffed and tied in a burlap sack, your beauty would still shine though."

I blushed through my running mascara. "I need to come here more often. You're good for my ego."

"Don't take my word for it, sweetheart. Just take note of how Biker Boy looks at you," he said.

"Oh, I'm sure he's just as sweet and charming to all the girls he brings around here," I said, rummaging through my purse for wipes, or sandpaper.

"Clutch? Out on the town charming the ladies?" Jimmy laughed so hard I thought *his* eyeliner might start running. "Oh, sweetie, that's good. I've never seen Clutch here for so much as a drink, since the day we opened."

"Really? He seems to like it, and knows so much about the place," I said, as I began the process of repairing the damage as best I could.

"Clutch may not be a regular, but there would be no Pink Priest without him."

"He mentioned that the club helped you set the place up."

"Not the club, honey. Clutch," he corrected. "Sure, the rest of the Burning Saints helped when it came to construction and the general cleanup of the surrounding area, but it was Clutch that led the charge."

"How so?" I asked.

"When this property came up for lease five years ago, Robert knew he wanted it. He'd been waiting for the perfect space to open his first restaurant for over a year, and we knew this was the place. We threw every penny we had into the business and had just started demo work when the trouble started."

"What kind of trouble?" I asked, turning to him.

"The hateful kind," he replied, looking down. "Within the first week after signing the lease, word got out around the neighborhood about what 'kind of place' the Pink Priest was going to be."

"Which was what?" I asked.

"A gay bar, a drag show, a bath house. Who knows what they thought? We heard all the theories and stories. Everything except the truth. Robert had a vision. The Pink Priest was to be a place where anybody could be themselves, free of any and all judgement. A gourmet dining experience where freaks and the "normies" could break bread, free of the persecution of the puritanical society we live in. I love Robert with all my heart and was determined to help him see his vision through. Some of our neighbors, however, had other plans." His tone was low and ominous.

"What happened?"

"One night, Robert was here working alone. He was doing some painting and three men in masks and hoods came in through the front door, which he'd propped open for ventilation. They snuck up on Robert and beat him with broom handles until he was nearly unconscious, tied him to a chair, and spray-painted horrible things all over the walls, and then on Robert himself." Jimmy's eyes filled with tears, and his voice began to waiver. "Then, they doused him with gasoline. They... were about to...to set him on fire when Clutch walked by and saw what was happening."

"Oh my God," I said, forcing back my own tears.

"He jumped in without hesitation and took on the guy with the lighter. Robert said Clutch knocked him out with a single punch before turning to the others. He said the three men never stood a chance. We never saw or heard from them again after that night."

"Not even in court?" I asked.

"There was no trial, honey. No arrest, no judge, and no jury. There was only Clutch."

A chill went down my spine.

"The next day, Clutch had a work crew here to help us finish the place, and the guys in the club have been our friends ever since. From that time forward, it became known around town that the Pink Priest was under the protection of the Burning Saints Motorcycle Club, and no one ever bothered us again."

"Under their protection? Why?"

"Because, that's the business the Saints are in. Didn't you know that already, sweetie? They protect people for money and hurt those that would try to hurt them."

"So, you pay him?"

He shook his head. "The Burning Saints have never asked us for a dime, and to this day, I don't know why Clutch did what he did. Like I said, he's never even been back since the grand opening, except to check up on us. He's never so much as asked for a beer on the house. Robert and I have tried to repay him in so many ways over the years, but he refuses every attempt. Your boyfriend may be a tough guy, but I see a good heart when I look at him, and I'm guessing you see the same thing when you look at him."

"He's not my boyfriend, that's for sure, and I haven't seen much of him at all lately," I said, returning to my feeble repair job.

"May I?" Jimmy asked, putting his hands out.

I gladly relinquished my make-up bag and turned toward him. Within two minutes he had me looking better than when I'd left the house.

"Holy shit!" I exclaimed, looking into the mirror.

"Okay, gorgeous. Let's go see if you can soften the boy's heart, and harden his—"

"Jimmy," I said, slapping his arm as we made our way out of the ladies' room.

* * *

Clutch

I glanced at my watch, then over to my only companion who, being a baked grouper, didn't have much to say. He (or she, I'm not sure) was a poor substitute for Eldie, who'd run out of the room over ten minutes ago. Jimmy had gone to look after her and had assured me he'd return her 'in two shakes of a lamb's fuzzy balls,' but so far, it was just me and the not-so-talkative fish.

What the fuck happened? Did I freak her out? I thought women were supposed to like it when men shared their feelings with them. Then again, Eldie wasn't like any woman I'd ever known, so maybe she'd rather me shut the fuck up and only concentrate on making her come. At least I knew I could make her feel good that way, and maybe that's all she wanted from me. Her leaving me alone with all these feelings and questions was driving me insane.

I'd long finished my fruity nightmare of a drink and was eyeballing the drink cart when Jimmy returned with Eldie, looking fresh as a daisy and as sexy as ever.

"You okay?" I asked, rising to my feet.

"She's fine, handsome," Jimmy said, replacing the lid on the grouper as he sat Eldie back down at the table.

"I'm sorry, I wasn't feeling very well, but I'm fine now," she said.

"Doc, if you're sick, we can take off right now," I said.

"I'm good. I want to stay, really. Maybe we could skip dinner and just talk?"

"Anything you want, Doc. You just let me know," I replied.

"I hope you're feeling well enough for one of Chef Robert's signature dessert creations," Jimmy said to Eldie. "They're quite impossible to resist actually."

"Oh, really?" she asked, shooting Jimmy an inquisitive look. "Well…maybe I'm feeling well enough for a few bites."

Clutch

JIMMY LEFT US, and I tried to get our conversation back on track.

"So, I kind of said a lot of things, and then Jimmy came in, and then you sort of ran out…" I said.

"Again, I'm so sorry about that," Eldie said.

"You don't have to apologize, Doc. I just wanted to make sure you heard what I said. About, you know, how I feel and everything," I said, finding it hard to keep eye contact. I hated this. I hated feeling weak in front of her. For some reason I wanted her to know that I was strong. I needed her to know that if she was with me, I'd always protect her.

What the fuck? If she was with me? What did that mean? Was I looking for a relationship with Eldie?

"Clutch?" Eldie waved a hand in front of my face, snapping me to attention. "You okay?" She chuckled.

"No...no Doc, I don't think I'm okay. I—"

"Hey," she said, taking my hands in hers. "It's okay, we don't have to talk about any of that right now. How about we get to know each other? Ya know, normal first date stuff."

"Chit chat?" I asked, raising an eyebrow.

"Sure, if you want to call it that." She smiled. "Let's start with something easy. Tell me about your family."

"Nothing to tell," I said.

"C'mon, they can't be *that* boring," she replied.

"No, I mean there's nothing to tell because there's no family."

"What do you mean?" she asked.

"No mom, no dad, no brothers, or sisters. No one else, just me."

"I'm sorry, I didn't mean to—"

"I was left at Firehouse Fifteen, wrapped in a blanket, stuffed in a duffel bag with a note that said, 'Please take care of my son. His name is Nikolai Christakos.' That's it."

"I guess that wasn't such an easy question to start with after all. I'm sorry."

"How could you know? It's no big deal anyway. Everyone has their own sob story, right?"

"Maybe, but that had to be difficult growing up without family or relatives of any kind," she said, with a heartbroken look in her beautiful eyes.

"I never really thought about it all that much, but it was tough sometimes when I'd meet another Greek person. They'd hear my name, or sometimes just take a look at me and say stuff like "Isn't it great to be part of the Greek family? Family this, and family that. Family, family, family."

"That must have been hard. I'm sorry."

"Was nine-eleven your fault too?" I asked.

"What?" she replied.

"I figured since you apologize for everything else, you must feel responsible for the attacks that happened on September the eleventh, two-thousand-one as well," I said.

"Bad habit, I know, saying I'm sorry all the time," she said sheepishly.

"I told you, Doc. You never have to apologize to me. I've done so much bad shit in my lifetime, I'm the last person on earth that deserves an apology for anything."

"You can't say that," Eldie said, sounding genuinely shocked at my words. "You were just a baby. No one deserves to start life out like that."

"Hey, I'm not saying I deserved being ditched, I just don't expect the universe to send me a great big apology over it. Plus, I've done enough bad shit to balance out what's been handed to me. Ya know?"

"No, I don't know," she replied.

"Here's how I see it," I said. "People are like machines, and they fall into one of three categories; in working order, broken but fixable, or fit for scrap."

"Sounds very scientific," she replied.

"Remember when I told you about Lucille? About how when I found her, she was just a rusted-out bucket of bolts?" Eldie nodded. "Well, whatever gift I have that allowed me to see that she was fixable also works on people. I usually know within moments of meeting someone which of the three categories they are in. I think the universe is constantly trying to balance everything within these three categories. You see it in nature all the time. Organisms that are healthy and thrive, and those that aren't either need to get stronger or die out and be recycled."

"I hope you don't take this the wrong way, but I'm not

sure that I would have pegged you as such a deep thinker," she said.

"I get it," I chuckled. "I guess you can blame Minus for some of that. I…I had a lot of spare reading time a while back, and he sent me a lot of great books. I read all of them and even understood half of them."

"So, what did you learn about yourself? To what do you attribute this so-called gift?"

"I believe it's my birthright," I said.

"What do you mean?" Eldie asked.

"I think that being born in the scrap pile gave me survival instincts that most people don't possess, and an insight to the world that is very cut and dry. It's what makes me really good at what I do."

"And what is that?"

"In the simplest terms, my job is to figure out if certain people can work productively with our club, can be made to do so, or need to be sent to the scrap yard."

"What does all of that mean?"

"Here's the deal, Eldie. I can't talk to you about my club's business, but we're in the confessional and I want to be honest with you."

"You can trust me with anything," she said.

"I believe you, but it's not that simple. We're not talking about my feelings anymore, we're talking about information that could send my brothers, or you, to prison. Worse yet, it could get one of you killed."

"Then why are you telling me this?"

"Because, I'm putting that life behind me," I said.

"You're going to leave the Burning Saints?"

"No. In fact, the entire club is going straight. No criminal activity and no more illegal business dealings."

"Wow, that sounds like quite a change from what I've heard about the Saints."

"That's all I can tell you right now, but I wanted to let you know that I'm trying to be a better man. For what it's worth."

"Can I ask you two things, and I promise I'll take whatever you say to my grave."

"You can ask, but I can't promise I can give you the answers," I replied.

"When you said that you had some 'spare reading time a while back,' does that mean you were in jail?"

"No, it wasn't jail. I was in prison. I did just over two years of hard time for aggravated assault."

She swallowed, then asked, "Have you ever killed anyone?"

I stared at her, careful not to make any expression at all. I searched my brain for precisely the right words to say, when once again the door flew open.

"Who's ready for dessert?" Jimmy's voice rang out.

* * *

Gina

As much as I wanted to know the answer, I was almost relieved when Jimmy came bursting through the door. This time with a dessert cart being pushed by a stout, unassuming man with a salt and pepper beard, wearing a black chef's jacket.

"How've you been, Bob?" Clutch asked, rising to his feet to greet him with a warm embrace, somewhat to my surprise. I suppose after meeting Jimmy, I'd assumed that someone named 'Robert the Oral' would be a lot more over the top, but this guy had about as much sparkle as a piece of toast.

"I'm doing fantastic, Clutch. Thank you for asking," Bob said softly before turning to me.

"I understand the fish wasn't much of a hit, so I hope our house specialty dessert makes up for it," he said sweetly.

"Oh, no. I'm sure the fish was lovely, I just—"

"It's perfectly alright, no need to apologize. We're just

so glad that you're here with us tonight."

"Your restaurant is amazing and beautiful. I've honestly never seen anything like it," I said.

"I guess you could say it was my vision and Jimmy's eye for...whatever the fuck all of this is," he said motioning all around.

"The televangelist trophy heads are my favorite," I said.

He patted his chest just over his heart. "Those have a special place in my heart."

"Why's that?"

"My family is super religious, and very conservative in their views. We went to church every Sunday morning and every Wednesday night. If there was a special service for any reason, we'd go to that as well. As the only son, it was my mother's greatest hope for me that I would become just like Pastor Ron. He was our church's new senior pastor, and hotshot preacher. When I was ten-years-old it was announced to me that I was to start saving a portion of my allowance every week in order to pay for Bible college. My parents told me that for every dollar that I saved, they'd double it. I did as I was told and by my seventeenth birthday, I'd surprised them by saving almost seven thousand dollars. I'd saved every penny I'd ever earned or gotten for my birthday. I became obsessed with making as much money as I could, so I'd be able to move off and go to school."

"You really wanted to go to Bible college?" I asked.

"Hell no, I wanted to move to France, go to culinary school, and fuck French guys."

"How did your parents take that news?"

"All I told them was that I wanted to go to culinary school, and that I'd like them to honor matching what I'd saved, as this was truly my passion and what I felt called to do with my life. My father then told me that he and my mother would never settle for me going into any field less than *the ministry*, especially one like the restaurant business, as it was so rampant with gays."

"He didn't!"

"*He did,*" Jimmy chimed in.

"My mother then told me she was going to increase my weekly sessions with Pastor Ron to twice a week, as I clearly needed guidance. I told her that sounded like a great idea."

"You did?" I asked.

"You bet I did. I loved giving head and Pastor Ron was hung like a mule."

Clutch laughed. "See? They don't call this the confessional for nothing, Doc."

Robert continued, "So, that was the day my parents found out their son was gay, and the day I found out they'd already given all my and my sister's college funds to the church; to help fund Pastor Ron's new TV ministry."

"So, you created this place," I said.

"That's right. I created this place as a fuck you to anyone who told me I couldn't, and a reminder to myself that I could. It's both sacred and profane to me, as are the people in it."

"It's beautiful."

"Thank you, sweetie, it was a pleasure meeting you. I hope you enjoy the rest of your evening."

"I'm sure we will. Thanks again, Bob," Clutch said with a wink.

"Now, on to dessert!" Chef Robert placed his hand on the handle of the silver dome, and I held my breath in anticipation for a repeat of the main course. I'd been traumatized by Indiana Jones and the Temple of Doom as a little girl, and for all I knew, there were chilled monkey brains under there. He lifted the lid to reveal a decadent chocolate masterpiece. It was truly a work of art and appeared to be made primarily from a familiar treat.

"Are those—"

"This is one of my signature creations, made by request for you this evening. This is my loving tribute to the greatest snack cake ever made, Mr. Winston's Chocolate Yum Yums," he said smiling.

Before us was a mountain of stacked Yum Yums, drizzled with layers of caramel, and chocolate sauce, surrounded in a whipped marshmallow mote. Throughout the mountain were caves which were each inhabited with scoops of various flavors of ice cream. It was as playful as it was elegant, and next to Clutch's naked body the most delicious looking thing I'd ever seen. In fact, at that moment, I didn't know which one I wanted to take in my mouth more.

"I can't believe you did this," I said to Clutch.

"Bob here made it, I didn't do anything," he replied.

"Thank you, Chef, it looks amazing," I said to Robert before turning back to Clutch. "I mean, I'm just touched that you did something so thoughtful in arranging all of this. Even despite my little spell earlier, this has been wonderful, especially you Jimmy."

"Jimmy is in the service of the Queen," he said with a slight bow, and with that the two men made their exit.

We returned to small talk while we ate dessert, and as we got up to leave, Clutch pulled me close for a deep, slow kiss. "I know we never finished our conversation and we will, but for now, I'd like to take you home and not talk for a while if that would be okay," he said.

"I'd like nothing more," I replied, and we got up to go, hand in hand. I'd slipped back into my cruel shoes but felt like I was walking on air. I'm sure it was a mixture of the sugar buzz and sexual high that was starting to come on, but I hadn't felt this great in a long time.

We made our way towards the exit, Clutch making me laugh with a running commentary on the restaurant's décor as we passed each piece. The cool night air was a soothing welcome to my warm skin. I was still a bit over-heated from getting ill but had almost returned to feeling normal. Since we'd driven here separately, Clutch was going to follow me home on Charlene. I was jealous that he got to ride her before me, but as long as he didn't make me wait much longer I thought I'd survive. We kissed and turned to walk in separate directions when I heard Clutch shout, "Shit! No!" and turned to see him running across the street. At first, I didn't see who or what he was running toward, but my heart sank when I realized what was happening.

"Mother fuckers! I'm going to rip your fucking heads off! Whoever did this is dead!" he yelled at the top of his lungs with unbridled rage.

I ran to Clutch, although I barely recognized him. It was as if he'd transformed into a different person. There was a disconnected look in his eyes, and his face was twisted into a sick half-smile. It was as if he was completely consumed by his anger.

Clutch stood in front of Lucille, or at least what remained of her. There didn't appear to be a single spot on the body that had not been dented, scratched, or punctured. The hood had been removed and the engine was covered in what looked like tar. Every window was completely shattered and on the roof the words "DEAD SAINT WALKING" were spray painted in bright orange. All four tires had been slashed and every light broken. As bad as all of this was, it paled in comparison to the interior, which was covered in what looked and smelled like blood.

"Clutch, I'm sorry—"

"Go home, Gina. Now. Don't stop for gas or groceries. Go straight home. Lock your doors and text me as soon as you get there," he said.

"Where are you going?" I asked.

"To look for who did this."

The tone in Clutch's voice and the expression on his

face answered my earlier question about whether he'd ever killed someone.

SIXTEEN

BURNING SAINTS

Clutch

I LEFT ELDIE at her Jeep and ran toward the rear lot where I'd parked Charlene. When I found whoever did this to Lucille, I was going to make him beg for his mommy. No fucking mercy no matter what the new rules were. He fucked with Lucille, my number one lady. I'd poured my heart and soul into her and he violated her. I was going to kill this bastard with my bare hands, and I was going to take my sweet time doing it.

As I rounded the corner, I could see a dually flatbed truck in the parking lot and two men attempting to load Charlene onto it. These must have been the same guys that trashed Lucille, and the flatbed was how they got her here in her condition.

I slowed my pace, pulled my gun, and moved in quietly for a better look. The parking lot, like much of Portland itself, was poorly lit, but as I got closer, I could clearly see that one of them was wearing a black hoodie with a white dragon.

The same motherfucker that was creeping around Gina's place.

Before I knew it, I was running full speed, straight at him. His partner saw me coming and took off, but I stayed on the Dragon, who'd turned to run, but was too late.

I leapt in the air and tackled him to the ground, pinning him to the asphalt with my full weight. I'd knocked the wind out of him, and he gasped for breath. I sat up and stuck my gun in his face while I grabbed his hood.

"Let me see your ugly fucking face before I put a hole in it," I said pulling back his hood. Instead of a hardened thug, looking back at me was a petrified kid, struggling for air. He was Hispanic, was certainly too young to vote. Shit, he barely looked old enough to shave. I holstered my piece and pulled the kid to his feet.

"You trying to steal my bike, you little fucker?" I growled at him as he continued to fight to breathe. I hit the skinny little shit with everything I had, my shoulder hitting him squarely in the solar plexus. "Did you trash Lucille, too? Were you the one who killed my fucking car?" I screamed, shaking the kid like a rag doll.

He was just about turning blue, when he finally gulped in enough air to squeak out, "They…made…me…do it."

I yanked him to his feet. The kid couldn't have weighed more than a buck thirty-five.

"Who made you do it? Who the fuck are you? Who told you to trash my car and steal my bike?"

"It was…my…initia…init…"

"Your initiation?" I asked, to which he nodded. "You did this to get into Los Psychos? You violated my Lucille, so you could run with those pieces of human shit?"

He nodded again, this time avoiding eye contact.

"Look at me, you stupid little punk," I barked. "I'm gonna give you one chance, and one fuckin' chance only to tell me every goddamned thing you know about Los Psychos. What the fuck they want with us, and exactly how you and your bitch partner are involved. 'Cause he's next on my list."

"He's was just trying to…get in like me. I swear to God."

"You don't swear to God," I said, pulling my 9mm out and pressing it against his forehead. "You swear to me. You're gonna tell me everything I want to know, or I promise I will kill you, and I will make your death slow."

I was still holding the kid by the scruff of his hoody and I felt his legs give out from underneath him. He didn't pass out, per se, but if I hadn't been holding him up, he would have dropped like a stone. The kid looked like he was gonna piss himself, so I holstered my gun and sat him down on the flatbed. He looked more like a childhood trauma victim than a hardened thug. Shit, he didn't even look like a softened thug.

At that moment, every ounce of fight I had drained out of me, as if someone pulled a plug to a reservoir in my body that had been holding it in all along.

"What's your name, kid," I asked.

"Alejandro."

"Alejandro, my name is Clutch, and I mean it when I say that I'll be the last person you ever meet if you try to run, draw attention to us, or otherwise escape. Do you understand?"

He nodded.

"Good, because you're coming with me right now and we're taking this Flatbed."

* * *

My prisoner and I arrived at the compound around one a.m., and I marched him to the bunkroom where the Peckers' were currently housed. I'd blindfolded Alejandro for the trip, as I still had no idea what I was gonna do with this fucking gangbanger wannabe.

"Get the fuck up, you've got company to entertain," I said barging into the room and turning on the overhead lights.

"What the fuck?" Big Pecker growled like a bear coming out of hibernation.

Little Pecker shot up in his bunk and cried out, "Mommy?" before collapsing and falling straight back to sleep.

"Oh, we're gonna talk about that shit later on," I said to no one in particular.

"Get the fuck up!" I bellowed even louder, this time bringing both men to their feet. "Good," I said. "Listen carefully. This is Alejandro, the Fuckface Kid. He's a dead man walking, and you two are gonna guard him until I get back."

"When will that be, exactly?" Little Pecker asked, to which I replied, "Not exactly sure."

"Approximately?" he asked.

"How 'bout this, Peckerhead. You and your large friend just be sure to guard him until I come to get him. Maybe that's in fifteen minutes, and maybe I'll be gone for two weeks. Either way, the mission is the same. Keep the fuckin' prisoner in this room and guard him until I get back."

The Peckers nodded, and I turned to leave, but paused to add, "Oh yeah, if he tries to escape, beat the shit out of him. Don't kill him, because if anyone gets to do that, it's gonna be me, but if he tries to run, feel free to make sure he never walks again."

I tasked two of the soldiers, who also lived on the

compound, to carefully get Charlene down off the flatbed. I'd had Alejandro help me load her on the back at the restaurant, under penalty of castration if he so much as breathed on her too hard in the process.

Once I was ready to roll, I texted Eldie but got no response. I called her, but after several rings it went to voicemail. I rode home frustrated that I couldn't get a hold of her. My reaction to seeing Lucille probably freaked her out for good and she was avoiding my calls. I figured I'd give her some space and try her again first thing in the morning.

* * *

The sunlight that poured into the room stung my eyes as I scrambled for my phone. It was 11:15 a.m., and Eldie still hadn't returned my call or text. I figured she was likely off and running early this morning and simply didn't check or respond to her messages. No worries, as I planned on swinging by the clinic on my way to the Sanctuary anyway.

I threw on the cleanest pair of jeans and black T shirt I could find. As I pulled the shirt over my head, I could smell Eldie's scent lingering on my clothes.

God, I miss her.

This was a feeling I was not at all accustomed to. I guess I missed Minus when he was sent to Savannah, but I was mostly able to block that shit out, as it was just as much business as it was personal. This was different. When Eldie wasn't by my side, I felt like a chunk of myself was walking around out there in the world without me.

I went to the kitchen to make some coffee. I'd managed to keep it as clean as Eldie had left it, which wasn't hard considering I lived on smoothies, grilled chicken breasts, and buffalo meat protein bars. I started a pot and texted Eldie while I waited for the machine's brew light to change from "Almost ready..." to "Enjoy!" Still no reply from the Doc, so once I'd finished slugging down my cup of jet fuel, I hit the road.

I pulled up to Eldie's clinic twenty minutes later to find the parking lot completely empty and the doors locked. I peeked inside and couldn't see any people or lights. I immediately dialed her number.

Straight to voicemail.

Shit. What the fuck was going on? Was she avoiding me after last night? Did the shit with Lucille scare her off for good?

She wouldn't shut her clinic down for the day if she was ghosting me. Something else was going on here and whatever it was wasn't good. If Los Psychos could snatch Lucille out from underneath me, maybe they did the same with the Doc. I got back on Charlene and sped off for the compound. If Los Psychos had anything to do with this, I was gonna get some answers from a certain punk car thief, regardless of whatever weird soft spot I had for him.

I arrived to find Minus, Ropes and Kitty talking with the kid in the great room.

"I told the Peckers to keep this little fucker on ice in their room until I got back, so which one of them do I get to beat the shit outta first?" I asked upon entering.

"Relax, I found out Alejandro was here, and brought him out to have a little chat," Minus said, in his signature slow and easy tone.

"Oh, good. I'm so glad you're all so relaxed because I have a question of my own," I said, yanking the kid to his feet and slamming him against the nearest wall. "Where the fuck is she?"

"I...I...don't know who you're talking about," he stammered.

"Clutch let him go. He's okay," Minus said, now on his feet.

"Bullshit *he's okay*. This little fuckstick is the one that took Lucille and now Los Psychos have kidnapped Eldie.

"I'm gonna pull his fingernails out one by one until he tells me where they're holding her," I said, pressing my forearm against the little weasel's scrawny neck.

"Listen, man," Kitty said. "For what it's worth, this kid started showing up right after I hooked up with Los Psychos. He ain't even a prospect. It sounds like he and his buddy boosted your ride just to get a foot in the door."

"Yeah, well I'm gonna take that foot and jam it right up his chicken ass unless he tells me every goddamned thing he knows about those psycho sonsofbitches."

"What exactly do you think we were doing before you got here?" Minus asked in a tone meant to yank my chain just a bit. I took the cue and relaxed my grip on the kid.

"Sit the fuck down," I barked, and he did as he was told. "Now speak."

"We were told to steal your car, trash it, and then do the same with your bike," he said.

"What about the Doc?" I asked.

"Who?"

"Gina, the woman I was with last night. Who took her and where do they have her?"

"I don't know anything about a woman, I swear. We were only told to fuck up your rides, that's it, I swear," he said, his voice cracking.

"You're gonna pray to God that he kills you if I find out that you're lying to me," I said. "'Cause I'm going to make this slow—"

"Jesus, Clutch. He's just a kid, back off," Minus said.

"Eldie is missing, and if I find out this little shit could have helped us, and he didn't—"

"What exactly do you mean she's missing?" Minus asked.

"She's vanished. She hasn't returned my calls or texts from last night, or this morning, and her clinic is a ghost town."

"That is strange. I've never known her clinic to be

closed on a weekday. She's even there most weekends, so that doesn't make sense," Minus said.

"That's what I'm saying. I don't like this man. I think Los Psychos fucked up Lucille to hurt me, and I'm afraid they're doing the same thing with Eldie. I've gotta find the Doc. Minus, I love her, and I won't be able to live with myself if anything happens to her."

* * *

Gina

Two days. I'd been hiding here for two days and I still hadn't come up with a plan. At least no one knew where I was. The last thing I needed was an interruption to my private meltdown.

I turned on the electric kettle and grabbed a mug from the cabinet, opening the pantry and stepping inside for a teabag. I couldn't believe my life had come to this. I'd greatly miscalculated my badassery and now I was paying for that mistake.

I was old enough to know better.

Shaking my head, I walked back into the kitchen and froze.

"What the fuck, Eldie?" Clutch growled.

The teabag fell out of my hand and I felt the light begin to fade.

"Doc? Fuck! Gina!"

Strong arms grabbed me as I lost consciousness and let the blissful nothingness take me.

"Baby," Clutch rasped. "Fuck. Eldie, I'm here. Let me help you up."

I found myself lifted from the floor and cradled against his chest. It took me a few seconds to fully comprehend my surroundings, but once I did, I shoved at his shoulders.

"What are you doing here? Let me go."

"I couldn't find you." He pulled me closer. "I thought they'd taken you."

"Who?" I pushed at his shoulders again, but he wouldn't budge. "Clutch let me go."

He shook his head and carried me to the sofa. "No. Never gonna happen again. Do you know what the fuck I've been through over the past forty-eight hours?"

"I've been here the whole time. I...I needed time to think, time to be alone," I said.

"I didn't even know *here* existed. Do you know what I went through to find this place? I called and texted over a dozen times, went by your condo, and everywhere else I could think of. I almost beat the shit out of a punk kid in order to find you. Why the fuck didn't you call me back?" he snapped, setting me on the couch.

"I don't get cell phone reception up here. It's one of my favorite things about it. Why didn't you just go by my clinic? My nurse or the locum tenens could have told you that I was out of town," I replied, finally gaining some distance when he stood to pace.

"The locum who?" he said, screwing up his face.

"The doctor I brought in to cover for me while I'm away," I explained.

"Doc, I went by your clinic four times and no one is there. It looks to me like the place has been closed for business since you split."

"What? That's impossible. I called Doctor Bleeker and he assured me he was free to cover me for the week," I said.

"A week? You were gonna take off for a week and not tell anyone?" Clutch shouted.

"I *did* tell someone. I told my nurse Maggie, the head administrator at my dad's facility, and Doctor Bleeker, who up 'til now, I thought was dependable."

"But you didn't think to tell me?" he asked.

"No, I *did* think to, but decided I didn't want to," I replied.

"And why the fuck not?"

"Because, you're part of the reason I'm out here at my father's cabin," I said.

"What the hell did I do?"

"I can't do this right now," I said, rising to my feet, but feeling suddenly queasy.

"Baby, please don't shut me out, talk to me," Clutch said, gently pushing me back onto the sofa.

"Don't call me that," I said, tears forming in my eyes, standing again and stepping around the sofa to put distance between us.

"Just tell me what I did wrong, and I swear I'll make it right," he pleaded, moving toward me as I continued my retreat.

"You can't *fix* this, Clutch. What I'm going through doesn't fall under your neat little three category theory."

"Please, Eldie, what have I done?"

"Everything, Nicky, you've done everything!" I stopped my retreat and broke down, falling into Clutch's arms momentarily, before pulling myself away and beating on his massive chest. "You've barged into my life and complicated every aspect of it, ruined my post-divorce plans, made me feel things that I was nowhere near ready to confront emotionally, and now…now…I'm pregnant."

Clutch

THE BEATING OF my heart now matched the rhythm of Eldie's pounding fists. Hours ago, I was afraid that I'd lost everything, and now the woman I loved was telling me that she was pregnant with my child.

"What? Are you sure?" I asked, unable to contain my ear-to-ear smile.

I was going to be a father. For the first time in my life, I was going to have a real family.

"I'm a doctor. I'm pretty sure I know how to administer and read a pregnancy test," she said dryly. "This would also explain the recent bouts of nausea, crying, and eating anything that isn't nailed down."

I threw my arms around her and pulled her in as tight as I possibly could, before letting go in a moment of panic. "Oh, shit. I'm not crushing the baby, am I?"

"I'm only three weeks along, it's not even a baby yet," she said stepping away.

"Bullshit. That's my kid in there and there's nothing in the world that could ever keep me from raising him…or her."

"Nicky, I came up here to decide what I'm going to do about all of this, and you being around is not going to make this any easier. So, now that you know I'm okay, can you please leave? I'll get a hold of Maggie and figure out what's going on back at the clinic and text you when I'm back in Portland."

"Shoot me a text? What the fuck are you talking about? This is *our* child we're talking about; our family."

"We are not, nor could we ever be, a family. You're a criminal, Nicky! A criminal who kills people."

"Wait, hold on," I said.

"No, Nicky. I won't hold on," she said. "You want me to use your real name? You want me to pretend we're back in the confessional? You want honesty? Well, here it is. You make me feel better than any man has ever made me feel in every way. When I'm with you, I feel confident, beautiful, and more alive than I've ever felt before, but that is a fantasy. This pregnancy is a wake-up call back to reality, and I can't have you muddying the waters of my decision making when it comes to my real life."

"How can this just be your decision alone to make? Don't I have a say? Gina, I love you and I want us to have this baby together."

"See Nicky, that's the problem."

"I don't understand. What problem?" I asked.

"That's the first time you've ever told me that you love me and it's only because I'm pregnant."

"What the fuck?" I said in a tone that was probably not as sensitive as it should have been given the topic of conversation.

"I'm not mad, just being honest," she said. "I don't expect anything from you and am prepared to take care of myself."

"What the fuck is that supposed to mean?"

"It means, we had a fling and I should have been more careful. I'm a doctor for crying out loud. How many women have I treated that got pregnant while on the pill?"

"It wasn't a fling for me, Gina. I told you that before. I also just told you that I love you. Didn't you hear me?"

"Didn't *you* hear *me*? I don't need you to tell me that you love me in order to make me feel better. I know who you are. I've seen glimpses of what you're capable of, and it scares the shit out of me. You just said yourself that you were terrorizing some kid just because you couldn't find me. How am I supposed to consider raising a child with you? Come on, *Clutch.* What kind of future are you picturing here? A little biker baby, wearing a miniature kutte, and riding a big wheel? Tell me, where do you see his father in this scene?"

"I see him right alongside his boy, teaching him to ride," I said.

"Let me tell you what I see," she said, looking deep into my eyes. "I see his father behind bars, or in the cemetery."

"I meant what I said before about wanting to be a better man and about our club going clean, and I opened up to you about all of that before I knew you were pregnant. I also told Minus that I loved you after you went missing. Gina, I was out of my mind when I thought you'd been taken from me. Now that I know that you're carrying our child, I'm even more committed to getting my shit together. I mean it."

"I don't know if that's enough. I saw true hate in your

eyes the other night. Murderous rage over a car, Nicky. I know Lucille was special to you, but what would you have done to the man that did that if you found him right then and there?" she asked.

"I did," I replied softly.

"What?"

"Just after I sent you home. I found him. He and one of his crew of wannabes had just dropped Lucille in front of the Priest for me to find her and were around the back trying to steal Charlene. It was the same guy that I was chasing that night around your condo."

"Who is he?"

"It was the kid."

"The one you said you almost beat up to find me?"

"I thought he was with a crew. Turns out, he's just some scrawny stray from the streets. The kind of kid that's a prime target for a gang or an MC to take in," I said.

"A club like the Burning Saints?" she asked.

"Worse, a club like Los Psychos," I replied.

"Who are they?"

"They are the people that I thought had taken you."

"Why?"

"Because that's how they do business. They were the ones that told the kid to trash Lucille. The kid was looking for a family, and they used him to get at me. Los Psychos takes the things you love and destroys them in front of you. They hate the Saints, and me and Minus are at the top of their shit list."

"So, let me guess. You were justified in doing to him what he did to your precious, stupid car."

"You can think what you want about me or my club, but you need to understand something. I have a code of ethics, and despite what you think you *may* know about me, there are lines I won't cross. My club gets physical, yes. And, to answer your earlier question, yes, I have killed people. Bad people, but I could never hurt a kid."

"You think, just because you deem your victims as bad, that gives you the right to commit murder?"

"I don't deem them as bad, Doc, their own actions do. I'm just the evil that finally catches up with them."

* * *

Gina

I'd taken a solemn oath to "do no harm," and I'd meant it with every fiber of my being. Now, a man that I'd only known for a few weeks, whose offspring was currently growing inside me, was admitting to committing multiple counts of murder.

"So, it's judge, jury and executioner for you, then? Your workday must be very busy."

"You know what? Maybe you're right," Clutch replied. "I have been paid to be all three of those things. Sometimes by good people, and sometimes by other criminals, but let me assure you that every single person I've ever put under the ground deserved the bullet they got."

"And what if you'd shot me the other night? Would I have deserved it?"

"That would have never happened," he said, taking a step toward me.

"Stay back, please."

"Gina, you don't ever have to be afraid of me."

"I *am* afraid of you now! You say that you couldn't have shot me, but the truth is you could have. One split second later and you could have killed me and our child."

"That's the first time you said, 'our child,'" Clutch said softly. "Baby, please give me a chance to show you that I'm done with that life."

"I told you not to call me that. Given my current condition, that word makes me extremely uncomfortable. I don't know why I said our child and I don't know what I'm going to do about anything yet. That's why I came up here in the first place. Now you've broken into my cabin, scared me to death once again, and confused me even more."

"I'm not confused. I love you and I want you, me, and this baby to be a family," he said taking my hands.

When he touched me, every part of me wanted to trust him; to believe him when he said that he could change, but even if he did, would that be enough? Even if the Burning Saints moved into owning and running legitimate businesses only, and Clutch became Nicky full time, he still had a past as checkered as they came. Was I going to spend the rest of my life looking over my shoulder like one of those Mob wives, waiting for him to get arrested for a crime he committed years ago? Even worse, what if I was arrested as an accessory after the fact? What would happen to Clutch, Jr. then?

On the other hand, I may be able to lie to Nicky, but I knew the truth, and that was that I'd fallen in love with him and wanted to have this baby more than anything.

"You have to go," I cried and broke away. "Please, just go home right now and give me time to figure everything out."

"After all of this, how can you expect me to leave you here now? I love you, Gina."

"If you really love me, then leave," I said.

Clutch's face was a stone. He said nothing, turned, and walked out, exiting the way he'd come in, silently. I heard the roar of Charlene's pipes as Clutch started her up, and as soon as they'd faded into the distance, and I couldn't hear them any longer, I cried and didn't stop for four hours.

EIGHTEEN

BURNING SAINTS

Clutch

I HIT THE bag with everything I had, throwing my full weight into each punch. Normally, I would classify what I was doing as "bad form," however, I wasn't currently focused on refining my right-hand technique, I simply needed to hit something, hard.

Eldie was right. I was a fucking animal that had no business raising kids, and a shit ton of nerve to try and convince her that I did. Not to mention, I didn't deserve a woman like her anyway. She said it herself. I was supposed to be a post-divorce hook up for her and my dumb ass went into the game ungloved. Now she's the one that has to pay the price.

The timer on my stopwatch chimed, signaling the end of this portion of my workout. It had been three days since I'd left Eldie at the cabin and wouldn't be surprised if I never heard from her again, which was probably all for the best. Minus had arranged for a sit-down meeting with Los Psychos' club President and I needed to focus on that. Easier said than done, but I was happy to have work to focus on. After what happened with Lucille, as well as similar damage to one of our downtown bars that was under renovation, Minus thought it best to arrange a meeting to air out whatever grievance their club had with us. Honestly though, the final straw was when those psychos threw a Molotov Cocktail at the building where Kitty used to live. Those pieces of shit had to know that he didn't live there anymore, or at least should have cared that families with children do. I hated these pricks and was pissed that they didn't get the message when we ran out their Portland Chapter President.

I crossed the floor of the Sanctuary's makeshift boxing gym to the speed bag. I tapped the bag with a firm, quick right, followed by a left, alternating hands until I found a steady rhythm as I thought about how everything around me had changed so suddenly. A few weeks ago, I thought that Los Psychos were in the Club's rear-view mirror, and that my biggest problem was whether Minus would let me open my gym. Now, the stakes had never been higher with Los Psychos as two club presidents were about to sit down for the first time. I'd potentially blown my one shot at becoming a father, and I didn't even have my fucking car anymore.

"Hey, yo. Can you do that Rocky shit?" a voice called out.

I stopped the bag and turned around quickly to see Alejandro, approaching with a mop and bucket.

"What the fuck do you want?" I asked.

"Nothin'. I just wanted to know if you could go super-fast on that thing like Rocky."

"Aren't you supposed to be cleaning this place up?" I asked our newest "intern."

"C'mon, man, I said I was sorry about your ride, and I'm gonna pay for all the repairs; every cent, I swear."

"Fuck off."

"I mean it. I'll work for your club for as long as it takes to make things right with you."

"Listen very carefully, you could never replace what you took from me in a million years, and just because Minus thinks it's a good idea to keep you around here, doesn't mean I do. In fact, if it was up to me, your ass would be out on the street for Los Psychos to deal with. I'm sure they'd be more than understanding about you failing to complete your mission, not to mention getting your ass captured by the enemy. Yeah, they seem like the real understanding types when it comes to shit like that."

He leaned against the mop handle sticking out of the bucket. "I told you guys that I don't want to go back to Los Psychos. The only reason I was with those guys in the first place was because of my friend Joe. He thinks he's a badass, so he wants to ride with them because they're all hard and shit."

"What about you, killer? You hard?" I asked.

"No," he said looking down at the ground.

"Let me ask you something kid. You got a family?"

"I got a sister," he replied.

"She with your folks?"

"No mom, no dad. Just my sister," Alejandro said without showing a trace of emotion.

"Well, I don't have a mom or a dad either. I don't even have a sister like you do. In fact, for a long time I didn't have anyone in the world that I truly loved, because they'd all abandoned me. Everyone except Lucille that is. No matter what, Lucille was always there for me, and the more love I put into her, the more love she gave me back in return. I loved her as much as anyone on this planet. Probably something close to how you feel about your sister, and now she's a barely recognizable hunk of twisted metal. Right now, my beloved Lucille is lying underneath a tarp like a dead body on a slab at the morgue, and you want to talk about repaying me?"

"I still hope you'll let me try," he said.

"Where is she now?" I asked.

"Who?"

"Your sister."

"Foster care, same as I was before," he replied.

"Before what?"

"Before I left, man, okay? They were gonna kick me out for fighting all the time, so I split."

"So, you *do* think you're hard?" I asked.

"No, but if someone's gonna come at me, I'm gonna defend myself."

"What the fuck do you know about defending yourself?" I asked.

"They had a punching bag and some gloves at one of the group homes I was in for a while. The guy that ran the place showed me a couple of boxing moves, and I kinda liked it. I was the smallest kid there, so I used to get picked on a lot. I started to fight back and most of the kids left me alone, but then I was in trouble with the staff, so I snuck out six months ago," he said, his eyes once again locked onto the floor.

Jesus, I'd have to be as blind and deaf as Hellen Keller, not to mention devoid of a heartbeat, not to see myself in this kid.

"The speed bag isn't about doing 'Rocky shit,'" I said, and Alejandro's eyes shot up to mine. "It's about finding a steady rhythm. Go get some gloves out of that locker over there and I'll show you."

* * *
Gina

I locked up my dad's cabin and headed to my Jeep. I didn't want to leave, but after driving into town yesterday so I could get a cell phone signal, I discovered Maggie had been left holding the bag, so to speak, since there was no doctor to cover for me. After being unable to get hold of me, she'd been forced to close the clinic until I returned.

It had been a tough few days, but I'd come to a decision and I was resigned to it. It wasn't an easy one, and I wasn't sure Clutch would let me put said decision into motion without giving me grief, but I was certainly going to give it a go.

* * *
Clutch

Sally Anne's was the designated spot for our meeting with Los Psychos, which felt poetic to Minus, as it was the place where we first encountered their club. However, it felt like a bad idea to me. I wanted to meet someplace out in the open, but even though we were co-owners in the place, Sally Anne's was still neutral territory, and Minus was betting on Los Psychos respecting that. I wasn't at all convinced and told Minus that I wanted to plant weapons around the place, just in case they tried anything.

"No, Clutch."

"Why the fuck not? I'm telling you, I don't trust these guys," I argued.

"You think I do?" he snapped. "The rules of the sit-down include no guns, no knives, nothing, and we're gonna honor the rules. Besides, you think they won't do a sweep of the room when they show up?"

"I don't like any of this and I'm going on the fuckin' record with that shit," I said.

"Duly noted, counselor," Minus replied with a smile.

"Listen up, Clutch," Warthog said. "From what I understand, El Cacto is as old school as they come and tough as fuck, so keep your quick mouth shut and let Minus and me do the talking, got it?"

I nodded silently, to which he replied, "Good."

"Where's the kid?" Minus asked.

"Ropes has him stashed in the keg room. He'll bring him out if we need to use him as a bargaining chip," Warthog said.

"You okay with that?" Minus asked me.

"What the fuck does it matter to me?" I asked back.

"I dunno. The kid's been following you around like a puppy since you brought him home, and you haven't swatted him away with a newspaper yet," he said.

"So, the fuck what? The kid's alright. What of it?" I shot back.

"Nothin', I just wanted to make sure that if we need him as leverage, one way or the other, that you'll be okay with losing your shadow, if need be."

"Whatever, man. I just want to get these assholes dealt with, and I'd feel a lot better if I had a fucking gun strapped under this table."

Twenty minutes later, El Cacto, the president of the Los Psychos Motorcycle Club had arrived, along with three members of his club, all of whom were soldiers. In fact, El Cacto (The Cactus) was the only Los Psychos officer represented, which I found odd. Before El Cacto would enter the main dining room, his crew insisted they be allowed to do a sweep of the room with wands, just in case we'd hidden any weapons.

"Sure, we've got nothing to hide," Minus said while side eying-me. I fucking hated it when he was right.

After the sweep was completed, an elderly man, who looked to be in his early eighties entered the room. He was dressed in all white, except for his kutte, which almost looked out of place on him. His hair and beard were stark white, and he wore a white fedora and walked with a cane. He looked far more likely to welcome us to Jurassic Park than start a turf war on the back of a chopper.

"Bienvenidos, El Cacto," Minus said, warmly greeting our guest.

"I want to sit down, I want a very cold glass of tomato juice, and then I want you to tell me why I shouldn't kill every single one of the Burning Saints," El Cacto responded in a thick Mexican accent.

We took our seat, ordered a round of drinks from Devlin, and El Cacto continued, "I came up here from Mexico because I want to put an end to all of this trouble," he said.

"That's good to hear, sir, because we want peace as well," Minus said.

"This is not true," El Cacto replied sternly. "You wish for Los Psychos to be out of Portland. You made this noticeably clear with my grandson, when you ran him out of town as a total disgrace."

"Viper was your grandson? I didn't know. I'm sorry for your loss," Minus said.

"I was the one who ordered his execution," he said, matter-of-factly. "He was my middle daughter's son. He was also an arrogant, hot-headed piece of shit, and a pain in my ass. I only gave him Portland because I don't care about it."

"If you don't care about Portland then why are you here? Why hire a tech expert to fuck with us and the Dogs of Fire? Why all the recent attacks on our club?"

"I'm here because I care about the reputation of the club that I founded. I'm focused on California, Nevada, and Arizona right now. That's where the money is for us. Portland makes a few dollars in meth, that's about it, but that's not the point. I can't have some club, that I've never even heard of, drive my boys out of a market, no matter its size. It makes me look bad, and it pisses me off."

"I understand, sir, but Viper came at us. We really had no choice but to handle him as we best saw fit."

El Cacto looked at Warthog and said, "I understand my grandson beat you."

"Nah. He was too chicken-shit. He hired someone else to do it," Warthog replied.

"I apologize. I never liked his methods, although they were effective from time-to-time."

"Viper turnin' up dead pretty much made us even, so I'm good," Warthog said.

"So, if you don't care about Portland, and you're not in mourning over your daughter's son's demise, I have to ask again, what it is that you want."

"All of these so-called attacks are a result of an inexperienced club, without a president, acting out without direction. I need to put a new Portland Chapter President in place, so I can rebuild and strengthen my club's presence here, and I need to know that you're not going to interfere."

"Let me get this straight. You want me to allow you time to strengthen your Portland club, so the next time they come after my club they won't fail?"

"Not allow. It's simply going to happen. Minus, the Burning Saints do not have the number or the resources that Los Psychos do. If I wanted to turn my resources toward wiping you out completely in Portland, I could do so."

"Don't be so sure, pal," I said, and Minus shot me a look.

"We could have an all-out war, or we could come to an agreement," El Cacto said.

"I'm listening," Minus said, calmly.

"Just as we once owned this very establishment, we will now own the protection business here in Portland, as well as retain control of all that we currently run. It's my understanding that your club is leaving the protection game, so it should be of no consequence to you."

"You're very wrong there. It's a big deal to me because I don't want someone coming in and squeezing my neighbors. We've always protected the people of Portland without bleeding them."

"It takes a lot of balls for a man to leave a woman and then tell the next man who comes along how he can treat her."

"We're not leaving Portland, just transitioning away from some of our former enterprises. That's all," Minus said.

"There's a lot more than that to your story and I know it. I also know that you can't afford a war, so my proposal is this; I appoint a new chapter president, recruit some locals, and assume your protection book. In return, I promise to run it fairly, and change none of the terms that you have with your existing clientele. Sound fair?"

"By recruiting locals, are you planning to continue to troll middle schools, for would-be car thieves?" I asked.

"I have no idea what you're talking about," El Cacto said.

"Oh, yeah? I caught a skinny little runt who stole and trashed my classic Barracuda, and he said your club recruited him to do it. I felt so bad for the kid I couldn't bring myself to toss him back to your wolves, considering what you did to Viper."

"You speak plainly, don't you?" El Cacto asked me.

"As plain as I like my burgers," I replied.

"You were right in not returning this boy to Los Psychos if you didn't want him hurt. A recruit that fails will certainly have to pay the price."

"You can let your crew know that the kid is staying with us, as well as Kitty, the tech specialist they hired. Any retaliation on them is going to be seen as a direct attack on the Burning Saints," Minus said.

"So, we have an agreement then?" El Cacto asked, rising to his feet, and extending a hand.

"If it means peace, then yes," Minus said, completing the handshake.

As soon as El Cacto and company were gone I turned to Minus. "What the fuck was that?" I asked.

"A peace negotiation, no thanks to you. What part of keep your fucking mouth shut during the meeting didn't you understand?"

"Peace? You showed him your neck and let him fuck the club in the ass."

"Clutch, as usual, what you don't know could—"

"I swear to God, Minus, if you even try to quote Cutter to me I'll burn this fucking place to the ground. I know you want us out of the muscle business but letting Los Psychos move in like this feels wrong."

"We don't have much of a choice unless you want all-out war, Clutch!"

"I'd rather go down with a fight than just give in to them."

"That's not what we're doing," Minus said.

"Well, it sure as hell feels like it. Jesus, Minus, how much more can I fucking lose?" I shouted and bolted out the door.

I rode straight to Eldie's clinic. I figured she had to be back by now and I couldn't wait for her to reach out any longer. I needed answers about our future, and I was really hoping that she had them.

NINETEEN

BURNING SAINTS

Clutch

I 'M NOT SURE who was more surprised when I burst into the exam room, Eldie, or the shriveled old man, whose balls she was currently cupping.

"Mr. Christakos, as you can see, I'm currently with a patient. Please wait for me in the *waiting* room, and I will be with you momentarily," she said, shooting me daggers the entire time, yet never taking her hands off her work.

"I'd love to wait, but I'm afraid you'll slip out the back, or shimmy down the drainpipe."

"This is a one-story building, so please leave this room and take a seat in the first floor waiting room!" she snapped.

"Ow!" her patient exclaimed.

"I'm so sorry Mr. Blondino, I didn't mean to squeeze you," she said before mouthing "get out" to me.

I went out to the waiting room and took a seat in one of the only available plastic blue and white chairs. From the look of things, Eldie's clinic operated on a tight budget and I got the feeling that most of her clients were not loaded with cash, as much as they were loaded on cheap vodka. Maggie, who I'd practically run over when I'd barged in, gave me the stink eye as I picked up a year-old copy of Golf Digest and pretended to read. After nearly ten minutes Eldie finally came out of the exam room, with her patient, who was now fully dressed.

"Just remember to be careful next time, Mr. Blondino," she said as she walked him to Maggie's desk, to check out. I stood up and she walked over to me, smiling the whole time before addressing the room full of waiting patients.

"I know you've all been waiting, and I'm deeply sorry for the delay. We've had a remarkably busy day with several unexpected *walk-ins*," she said glaring at me. "If you'd just allow me to speak with this patient for two minutes, I promise we'll get right back on schedule," she said, pulling me by the elbow back into the exam room.

"What the hell do you think you're doing, barging into my clinic and interrupting a hernia examination," she asked.

"Oh, shit is that what that was? Thank God. I thought I had some competition for a second," I teased nervously.

"This is not a joke, Clutch. I could lose my medical license over incidents like that. The people in this community depend on me. Not that anyone around here could tell these days, thanks to the shitty job I've been doing. It's become painfully clear to me that I need to focus more on my work and less on running around with bikers making stupid decisions."

"Speaking of. Have you made a decision about the baby?"

"Yes, I have, as a matter of fact, but I don't think you're going to be happy about it," she said.

My heart felt like it was being squeezed, and I thought I might throw up right then and there.

"So, you're not going to have the baby then?" I asked.

"No. I *am* going to have the baby, but I don't want you to be the father," she said.

"That's not really how it works though, is it, Doctor?" I asked, confused as to what the fuck she was saying.

"Well, it's how *this* is going to work. I'm going to give birth and raise this baby, and I don't want you to be a part of its life or my life in any way," she said in a clinical tone.

"There's no way I can do that, Gina. After everything I've told you about my family history and about how I feel about you, how can you think that I could ever be okay with this?"

"I don't need you to be okay with it, I just need you to keep me and the baby safe by staying away from us."

"I can't do that, and there's no way that you're safer without me than you are with me," I said.

"You and I both know that isn't true. You are the Sergeant at Arms of a 1% motorcycle club. Just because Minus has big plans, and you agree with his vision, doesn't mean that *we* are anywhere near safe," Eldie said, rubbing her stomach.

"I just need you to give me a little time, and we're gonna get everything worked out, you'll see."

"I believe that you want to become a better man, but I'm sorry Clutch, that's not good enough for this, or any other child. I didn't plan on getting pregnant. In fact, I planned on never being pregnant, thus my being on the pill, but things happen, and plans change. So, even though I'm terrified beyond words, I'm going to have this baby;

and if I'm going to bring another child into this world, I have to do what's best for them, including making sure their father is a good man, not a hopeful criminal."

Eldie opened the exam room door wide. "Now, if you'll excuse me, as you can see, I have a lot of patients that need my attention."

I walked out of the room, stopping, and turning at the last moment. "I love you, Gina. I love you and our baby, and I always will. I'm gonna prove that to you."

"You can prove it to me by walking out the door and never coming back," she said, obviously trying to bite back tears.

My heart was pounding, and my head felt like it was on fire. My whole life, all I ever wanted was to have a family, and now to be so close to that dream becoming a reality, only to have it taken away at the last moment, was too much to bear. There was no way I was going to let them slip away, no matter what I had to do.

I said nothing more but knew exactly what I had to do.

I got back on Charlene and pulled out my cell phone, as I had a few calls to make before hitting the road. "Hey. Where are you? Can you meet at the Sanctuary in two hours? Alright, I'll see you then."

I hung up the phone and dialed the next number.

* * *

Gina

The look in Clutch's eyes when I told him to leave almost broke me. I hated lying to him and even worse, I hated lying to myself, and I was doing both when I told him that I didn't want him to be the baby's father. Of course, I did. I wanted nothing more. Clutch was the baby's biological father, and I loved him, but neither of those things mattered more than the fact that he would never leave his club, and his club would never be a safe place for our family.

The worst part of all of this was not knowing which of my emotions were being ruled by my heartbreak, and which ones by hormones. I think most of me was still in shock that I was pregnant in the first place. I honestly could not figure out what was wrong with me. Not wanting children practically destroyed my marriage, and now an unplanned pregnancy has me devastated about telling my biker baby daddy to hit the road.

What the actual fuck, Gina?

I knew it wasn't all about Clutch though, and that's what scared me the most. I had to be honest with myself and admit that I wanted this baby. With or without Clutch, or any man, I wanted this baby. I don't know what changed in me exactly; it was probably a lot of things, but I had profoundly changed.

It was hard for me to imagine how I'd felt before. The emotions behind not wanting children had all but vanished, and I somehow no longer felt afraid, even though I was scared to death.

Perhaps, I could just never see having a family with *David*, or maybe becoming pregnant flips some sort of internal "mom switch" that was hidden deep inside me. I'm not sure, but I knew without a shadow of a doubt that I wanted Clutch's child but was determined to protect him from his father's lifestyle.

"If we keep up this pace, maybe we'll get out of here by nine o' clock," Maggie said, in a cheerful yet exhausted tone. "I'll put on another pot of coffee while you see your next patient."

Maggie really had been my rock over the past few years, and I honestly don't think I could have kept the clinic running without her. She wasn't just the clinic's nurse. She ran the front office and sometimes spent more time with the patients than I did.

"Thanks, Mags. You're the best," I said before taking Mrs. Gordon back for her exam.

This is how I was gonna get through this. I was going to bury myself in my work right up until it was time to deliver the baby. Then I'd take maternity leave. Four days, a week, tops. I'd already have childcare worked out in advance, so when I went back to work it'd be no problem. Then I'd pick the baby up, go home and take care of it, then off to bed. Alone, without Clutch. Probably exhausted beyond all words, only to wake up and face another day of feeling guilty about being a single, working, mother who's allowing a stranger to raise her bastard child.

I may have been spiraling.

Is that coffee ready yet?

* * *

Clutch

"You're out of your fucking mind! That's it, Clutch. You've really gone all the way off the motherfuckin' deep end this time. There's no other explanation," Minus shouted as he paced his office floor.

"Love."

"What the hell are you talking about? Love? With a woman you've been with for a month? How is that not crazy talk, man?"

"It's not just about her, although I'd still be making the same decision even if it was."

"This is not right, Clutch."

"I called the officers and told them all to meet us here at ten o' clock," I said.

"Goddamnit, Nicky."

"I've made up my mind, Minus. I'm choosing Gina and I'm choosing my family, and I'm willing to do whatever it takes to get them back."

Gina

Miraculously, I was able to catch up on my patient load and close the clinic by a little after nine forty-five when I received a call from an unknown number. I answered the phone and was surprised to hear Cricket's voice.

"You need to go to the Sanctuary now," she said the moment I answered.

"Cricket? What's going on?"

"Gina, get to the Sanctuary right now. It's Clutch."

The tone in Cricket's voice caused me to hang up immediately and drive faster than I'd ever driven before.

TWENTY

BURNING SAINTS

Clutch

MINUS, ROPES, WARTHOG, Elwood, Mayday, and Wolf stood in a circle around me. The great hall was dark, except for light from a single lamp and the glow of a two-inch piece of steel that had been heated with an acetylene torch to over 500 degrees Fahrenheit.

Minus cleared his throat before speaking, "The Burning Saints have gone through a lot lately. Cutter dying, me becoming president, everything that went down with Grover and Los Psychos. Not to mention the shit I've been putting all of you through lately with the club's change in direction. It's been...well, a lot." Minus walked to me and put his hand on my shoulder, pausing briefly before continuing, "This isn't my choice, this is Clutch's. A Burning Saint has never voluntarily patched out of the club, but Clutch has assured me that he's made up his mind, and that his decision is final. He also understands that patching out means removing all club ink." Minus, turned to me and pleaded, "Jesus, Nicky, please don't do this. You don't have to. I can grant you mercy."

"I have to, or the club will never respect you. You stood up to Wolf in front of everyone and told him the only way out of this club was with the brand. If you go light on me, they'll never see you as a man of your word. If I go, my wings go, that's the law," I said.

"I can't do it, Nicky," Minus said, tears forming in his eyes.

"Make Wolf do it. He'll probably enjoy it," I laughed softly.

Minus nodded to Ropes and Elwood and they each took hold of one of my arms. Fortunately, I only had one club tattoo. It was my only tattoo in fact. Minus and I had gotten the same one, but on opposite sides of our chest, the very day we patched in. To me, it was my family crest.

Mayday gave the brand a final hit with the torch and handed it to Minus.

"C'mon man don't be a pussy," I said, but instead of taking the bait, Minus just stood there. Looking like he was gonna be sick.

"I swear to you, brother, this is what I want," I said softly. "The only way Gina is going to know that I'm ready to be a father and a husband; the only way I can show her that she and the baby are the most important things to me, is to let go of everything that stands in our way. I have to leave my old family behind in order to have any kind of chance with my new family. My *true* family."

Minus' eyes met mine, and the brand hit my chest.

The putrid smell of burning flesh penetrated my nostrils and my hands and feet contracted into tight balls as I screamed in agony. I had only moments to collect my thoughts before the bar was pressed, once again, against my bare skin. Ropes and Elwood supported my weight as I spasmed in pain, before blacking out.

Eldie yelling, "What the fuck is wrong with you people?" and the sound of clanking metal were the first two things I heard when I came to.

* * *

Gina

Cricket pulled up to the Sanctuary just as I was arriving. I parked diagonally over the lines, flung my car door open and practically lunged at her as she exited her car.

"What the hell is going on? Where's Clutch? What's wrong?"

"Eldie, Clutch is patching out tonight," Cricket said in a tone that sounded far too serious too me.

"What? What the hell? I thought Clutch had been in an accident or something," I said, annoyed that Cricket had gotten me worked up. Although, it was strange that the mere possibility of Clutch being hurt sent me hurtling toward the very people I wanted to avoid.

"I don't think you understand Eldie. Clutch is *patching out*. That means he's leaving the club."

"Clutch is leaving Portland?" I asked, my heart now feeling like it was lodged in my throat.

"No, Eldie. He's leaving the Burning Saints, forever."

I giggled nervously. "Nooo." I said, smiling. "Minus and the Burning Saints are his family. They're all he ever talks about. He'd never leave."

"He told Minus that you and the baby are his only family now, and that you're his only priority."

"He told Minus that?"

"Yes, Eldie. He's patching out for you. He wants to prove what you and the baby mean to him."

"Oh my god." I burst into tears. "I love him so much. I can't believe he would do that for me, for us."

"Eldie," Cricket said, directing my focus back to her. "Patching out means branding off his Burning Saints tattoo."

"What? Would Minus actually do that?" I asked, shocked.

"That's the law. I know Minus doesn't want to, but Clutch insisted it be done."

"That's crazy. Why would Clutch put himself through all of this?"

"I don't know, but if we can find them maybe you can stop him before it's too late."

I followed Cricket as we made our way inside and the smell of burning flesh assaulted my nose.

Ropes and Elwood held Clutch up as Minus pulled a hot iron away from Clutch's chest and he went limp. I made a running leap for Minus, hitting him as hard as I could in the jaw, causing him to stagger back.

"What the fuck is wrong with you people?" I screamed, wrapping my arms around Clutch as he started to come to. Ropes and Elwood helped to steady him, so I could check out his wound while Cricket tended to her man. "What have you done?" I growled at Clutch. "Someone needs to get my bag out of my Jeep."

"Big Pecker," Cricket directed, as I lifted Clutch's head.

"Hey, beautiful," he rasped.

I stroked his chin. "What are you doing, Clutch?"

He gave me a goofy grin. "I'm making you my priority."

I blinked back tears. "Nicky."

"I love you, Gina."

"I know."

"I'm gonna prove I'm worthy of you, baby. Both of you." He swallowed, grimacing as he pulled his arms from

Ropes and Elwood's hold. "Even if it takes me the rest of my life. I'm gonna prove it."

Big Pecker returned with my medical bag and I took the distraction, rummaging through it to find salve, gauze, and tape. Despite my watery eyes, I bandaged Clutch's wound and cupped his cheeks before rising to my feet.

Minus held a hand to his cheek and Cricket forced him to sit in one of the chairs next to the pool table. "What is it with you ladies punching me in the face?" I heard him say as he took a seat.

"Everybody listen up!" I bellowed, then slipped my finger and thumb into my mouth and let out a whistle no one could ignore. "Shut the fuck up!"

All eyes were suddenly on me and I crossed my arms and glared at each one of them.

"I have never seen a bigger group of idiots in my life," I ground out. "All of you are nothing more than ignorant assholes, and I'm over it. All of it!" I threw my arm toward Clutch. "This man is your *brother*! But you're all standing here, just watching as Minus shoves a hot poker against his skin to burn any memory of you away. None of you is objecting. None of you is standing up for him. None of you is man enough to do the right thing. I'm disgusted."

"I tried talking some sense into him. Believe me, none of the members want him out of the club!" Minus protested.

"But you mutilated him anyway, didn't you? Why? Because some douchebag tough guy with a handlebar mustache wrote a rule down in some book back in nineteen seventy-three?"

"Eldie," Clutch warned.

"You shut your mouth," I snapped. "You're the biggest idiot of them all, Clutch. God! I can't believe you'd do that to yourself! You could have died."

"I was in no danger—"

"Let me tell you where you're wrong, Nicky. You

could have gotten an infection in the wound, this could have spread to the rest of your body, not to mention your bloodstream, where your body could go into sepsis and then death. This whole practice is barbaric, not to mention stupid."

Clutch rose to his feet and made his way toward me. I wrapped my arms around myself as my body started to shake without warning. Clutch pulled me close and kissed my temple. "Come with me, baby."

He guided me out of the Sanctuary and into one of the private rooms where he wrapped his arms around me and pulled me close. I sobbed into his chest, careful to avoid his wound, and burrowed into the warmth of his body as he whispered sweet promises to me and our unborn child.

"Shh, baby, I've got you."

"Why would you do that to yourself?"

"It's part of our code. Part of our culture, Eldie."

"So is female circumcision in Somalia…doesn't make it right."

"I don't think you can compare this to that kind of mutilation."

I met his eyes. "You don't think so?"

He smiled, cupping my face. "I'm serious, Gina. I will give all of this up if it means I have any chance with you."

"Apparently." I slid my hand to his neck. "What am I going to do with you?"

"You're going to marry me and have my baby."

He was right. I was. But he didn't need to know that just yet.

"How are we going to make any of this work?" I whispered.

"How does anyone make it work, baby? We put one foot in front of the other and figure it out."

"I need you to promise me you won't kill anyone ever again."

"I promise."

"No beating anyone close to death either."

He slid a lock of my hair behind my ear. "I'm workin' on my anger issues, Eldie. Gonna prove that to you, I just need you to give me a chance."

I bit my lip and stared at him for several seconds. "I love you. More than I'm probably willing to admit. I think that's why all of this is so scary."

"I get it, Doc, but we're in this together. I love you and I promise I'll be the man you and our kid needs. I love you, Gina."

"I love you, Nicky," I said, and he kissed me with more than I'd ever felt him, or any man give me. Somehow, even amidst this strange chaos I knew I was in the safest place I could possibly be.

TWENTY-ONE

Gina

"**I** STILL CAN'T believe you actually bought us tickets to the theater," I said, taking off my heels.

"I told you I'm willing to try new things," Clutch said, smiling as he hung up our coats.

"So, you liked it?"

"I liked seeing you in that dress," he replied. "And now I'd like to see you out of it," he said, kissing my neck. Clutch led me to his bedroom and wrapped an arm around me, kissing me gently. "I got you something."

I raised an eyebrow. "You did?"

He grinned, grabbing a wrapped box from his nightstand and handing it to me.

I ripped it open and smiled slowly. "Clamps? You bought me clamps."

"I bought you the best fuckin' nipple clamps on the market."

"Really?"

He nodded. "Hatch's woman used to sell these."

I widened my eyes. "You asked Maisie what clamps you should buy me?"

Clutch laughed. "No, baby. I asked Cricket what it was like working for Maisie back in the day and the conversation kind of organically went there."

I blushed. "Does she…?"

"No, I didn't tell her anything."

I handed him back the clamps and pulled off my shirt and bra. I held my hand out, but he shook his head.

"Let me." He kissed me and then rolled my nipples between his fingers before securing each clamp and tightening the little screw. "How's that?"

"More," I said, my body already on fire.

He tightened them more and I groaned, reaching for his jeans and undoing the fly. I slid my hand under his waistband and wrapped my hand around his already hardening cock.

"Jesus, Eldie," he rasped, tugging gently on the chain between the clamps.

I groaned, kissing him again.

Pushing my jeans and panties from my hips, I grabbed his hand and guided it between my legs. "Feel what you do to me."

"Total perfection," he whispered, and kissed me again.

Lifting me onto the bed, he laid his palm to my chest and held me where he wanted me, kneeling between my legs and covering my core with his mouth. I squirmed against him and he raised his head with a frown. "You keep squirmin' like that, I'm gonna tie you to the bed."

I licked my lips and begged, "Tie me."

He grinned, stepping off the bed, and heading into the closet. He brought back two of his belts and ran the end of one across my belly. "Head on the pillows, Doc."

I shifted so my head was up by the headboard.

He tugged me down a little and took a nipple, clamp and all, in his mouth. He pressed the clamp tighter with his teeth and I felt the heat pool between my legs. My pregnancy hormone laced nipples were ultra-sensitive and I thought for sure I'd come right then and there.

He secured one wrist to the headboard and then the other and I tested its strength.

"Too tight?" he asked.

I shook my head, and he pushed off his jeans and knelt between my legs again. This time, he lifted my hips and slid into me, falling over me and covering my mouth with his. I wrapped my legs around him, the only way I could touch him.

Clutch broke the kiss with a grin, sliding out of me and then in again slowly. Then he moved faster, rocking into me as he tugged on the chain between my clamps and I hissed with need. He was going far too slow. I lifted my left leg, so I could control my lower body and arched against him.

He tugged on the chain again, sending a shot of desire between my legs again.

"Yes," I breathed. "Faster, Nicky."

He cupped my bottom and squeezed. "You want it harder?"

"Yes," I panted.

He smacked me, and I threw my head back with a sigh. For the next several minutes, he tugged, slapped, and drove into me while I came apart in his arms. His final thrust, combined with pulling the chain down, and I shattered.

Clutch released me from my ties and I wrapped my

arms around his neck and sobbed into his neck.

"Shit, baby, did I hurt you?" he whispered, pulling me close.

"No. It was amazing," I whispered. "Oh, my *god*, it was amazing. I think I'm just pregnant and hormonal."

He chuckled and held me tighter. "I love you, baby."

"Love you back."

He removed one clamp, sucking gently on my nipple, then did the same to the other. "How do they feel?"

"Like we're gonna use them every time."

Clutch laughed and climbed from the bed. He put the clamps back in the box and slid them back into the nightstand. "If we keep goin' like this, we're gonna need an extra closet. A drawer ain't gonna cut it."

"Technically, I really only need your dick."

He slid back onto the bed and kissed my belly.

"How many kids do you want?" I asked.

"As many as you want to give me," he said. "But we can start with this one and go from there."

I rolled onto his chest and kissed his neck. "I like that answer."

Clutch pulled the covers around us and settled his hand on my bottom. "Love your ass, Eldie."

I wrapped my hand around his hardening cock. "Love your dick, Nicky."

He grinned. "It loves you back."

"Prove it."

"Again?" He pushed me onto my back. "You act like you're tryin' to get pregnant or something."

I giggled as he shimmied under the blankets and kissed my stomach. He kissed one breast and then the other before moving between my legs.

"I want you to act like you need to put another baby in me," I demanded.

Clutch pulled the covers down, so I could see his face and grinned. "Your wish is my command."

As he worshiped my body all over again, I realized just how much I loved all of this. All of *him*. Good and bad. He loved me with everything he had, and I was damn lucky to have his adoration. He might be working to prove his worthiness to me, but the truth was, I had just as much work to do to prove my worthiness back to him.

Lucky for me, we had our whole lives in front of us and I couldn't wait to see what the future held.

Clutch

Three years later…

"USE THE JAB, use the jab!"

I wasn't sure if he was battling nerves, or if he couldn't hear me through the deafening crowd noise, but Alejandro "The Kid" Christakos, was gonna be kissing the canvas for the first time ever if he didn't start listening to my instructions.

Ding, Ding.

The bell signifying the end of round one sounded, and I set Alejandro's stool in the corner of the ring.

"Deep breaths," I said. "Remember to regulate your breathing between rounds," I instructed my young fighter.

"He hits a lot harder than me," Alejandro said, between breaths.

"Maybe he does, but you're faster and slicker, son, so use your jab. Stick that left-hand directly in his face and leave it there if you have to. Impose your will on this guy. Use your jab to control his distance. Then, once you've got him within striking range, unleash that right hand. But until then, I want to see you stick to throwing the left."

"Yes sir."

"You're not a caveman, so put away your club. Anyone can fight, we're here..."

"To box," he said.

"That's right. Now go show him who's got more heart, brains, and good looks than him," I said, smiling, and the bell rang.

I looked down to Eldie, who sat in the front row with our *three* daughters. That's right. In addition to Alejandro, whom we officially adopted three months ago, along with his sister Celia, Eldie gave birth to our beautiful twin daughters, Lucille and Charlene. Lucy and Charlee waved to me, their noise canceling headphones almost bigger than their tiny heads and I grinned, blowing them each a kiss. In one year, I went from a man with no family, to one with four kids and a beautiful wife. I felt as if I was living someone else's life sometimes. A better life.

Clutch Combat Sports was bigger and better than I could have ever imagined. We had three top level MMA and boxing coaches on staff, a full teaching schedule, and had been hosting monthly fights for six months. We even had yoga classes.

Neighborhood kids started pouring in once the Kid started making a name for himself. He was a natural, and his outgoing personality made him a great neighborhood ambassador for the gym and the club.

Club life had been a little trickier to navigate. Even though I was technically the club's Sergeant at Arms, I often played the role of Vice President. If Minus wasn't available and a club decision had to be made, he trusted me to make it. Cricket sat in the co-captain chair on business matters and I served as Minus' second on club matters. My role as pseudo-VP demanded a lot more of my time, as did my club schedule in general now that we were fully legitimate and functioning as a true business. After my failed attempt to patch out, I was surprised by the reaction of my brothers. I expected them to view me as a quitter after that, but the exact opposite happened.

Minus, and the others, recognized what I'd done was not about leaving the club, but about remaining loyal and true to my family. It was clear to me that these were the very traits the club had always valued.

Balancing family life with all of my other new responsibilities was a challenge, but I'd quit drinking, had never been in better shape, in every way, and barely even recognized myself sometimes.

Eldie smiled at me and I focused back on the ring. The two young lightweights circled each other in the ring, the Kid now extending his left far out in front of him, his opponent, moving back and forth in a frustrated attempt to work his way to the inside. Alejandro sticking him with a stiff jab the moment he stepped inside his range.

"There you go!" I yelled as the crowd erupted.

The Kid circled left while throwing two more quick jabs, momentarily stunning the other fighter, before releasing a clean uppercut straight up the middle, sending him backwards and straight to the canvas.

The ref began his count but waved his arms at seven when it was clear the other fighter was in no condition to continue.

I shot through the ropes, into the ring, and hugged my son, hoisting him onto my shoulders.

"You did it! I told you that you were gonna win. I'm so proud of you!"

The ring filled with our young fighters as they poured in to congratulate both fighters on a job well done. Alejandro was carried off like a hero, and I looked down once again to my ring-side bride, wondering what I could have possibly done to deserve such an amazing second chance at life.

If I thought Eldie was the most amazing woman I'd ever met before, I had no idea until I saw her become a mother. She swore up and down that she never wanted kids before she met me, but I'm not buying it. I'd never seen a more attentive and loving mother and seeing her with the kids only made me love her even more. I couldn't wait for our daughters to learn how to be strong women from her, and hopefully they'd learn a few things from me, too. So far, I think I've been the one to learn the biggest lesson out of all this; a lesson about happiness.

I always thought that I could never be happy, because I didn't deserve happiness, but the truth is, no one deserves happiness. But sometimes, if our hearts are open, we find it anyway.

I guess the trick is to recognize the people that we want to grow for, and maybe it's through that growth process that we find what we truly need to be happy.

Then again, maybe I was just the luckiest bastard in the world.

TRIXIE SUNRISE

BURNING SAINTS

Ingredients:
1 oz Patron Silver Tequila
1 oz Sailor Jerry Spiced Rum
4 oz Orange Juice
1 oz Lemon-Lime Soda
Grenadine syrup
Cocktail sugar

Instructions:
Sugar the rim of a Collins glass
Fill 2/3 with cubed ice
Add the Tequila, Rum, Orange Juice, and Lemon-Lime Soda
Top with a tiny splash of grenadine

Warning: Do not drink if you are pregnant, secretly pregnant, or planning on becoming secretly pregnant. Be sure to use caution as two or more Trixie Sunrises may cause you to engage in unusual or potentially risky behavior such as (but not limited to) having sex with a biker or mistaking your usually mild-mannered self for a "Badass Biker Bitch." Be sure to ask Jimmy if the Trixie Sunrise is right for you.

ABOUT JACK

BURNING SAINTS

USA Today Bestselling Author Jack Davenport is a true romantic at heart, but he has a rebel's soul. His writing is passionate, energetic, and often fueled by his true life, fiery romance with author wife, Piper Davenport.

Twenty-five years as a professional musician lends a unique perspective into the world of rock stars, while his outlaw upbringing gives an authenticity to his MC series.

Like Jack's FB page and get to know him!
(www.facebook.com/jackdavenportauthor)

Made in the USA
Coppell, TX
13 February 2023

12683044R00115